THE BRAIN DRAIN

Sara recovered consciousness to a sort of swaying motion. She opened her eyes and saw corridor walls going past. She was being carried somewhere on a stretcher. But why?

She was lifted from the stretcher and placed on a table. An operating table, thought Sarah wildly. She'd been hurt in an accident and now they were going to operate. She was in a small circular room that was packed with complicated equipment. Lights flashed before her eyes, and there was a low background of electronic hums and beeps.

A face appeared, hovering above her. It was Harry. Good old Harry Sullivan. Naturally, he'd be there if she'd been hurt.

"Harry?" she whispered weakly. Sudden panic swept over her and she started to struggle. But she couldn't move—there were clamps holding her to the table.

Harry moved away and a moment later another face appeared. It seemed strangely distorted, and Sarah blinked furiously, forcing herself to concentrate. As her vision cleared, she gave a gasp of pure horror. The face hovering over her was broad and flat with leathery greenish skin. The hideous vision loomed larger—then Sarah slipped into unconsciousness.

The voice of Harry Sullivan said impassively. "She is ready, Styggron."

"Good. Commence the analysis of the brain."

THE FOURTH DOCTOR WHO

This episode features the fourth Doctor Who, who has survived three incarnations. The long trailing scarf, the floppy wide-brimmed hat, the mop of curly hair and the wide-eyed stare—all these are the obvious trademarks of the fourth Doctor Who. Along with a delightful mix of personality traits: genius and clown, hero and buffoon—the fourth Doctor Who combines the best of all who preceded him.

DOCTOR WHO'S COMPANIONS

SARAH JANE SMITH

Sarah is an independent freelance journalist. She has a mind of her own and once, while in search of a story, stowed away on Doctor Who's TARDIS—and ended up in the medieval past. Forever swearing she will never again set foot in the TARDIS, Sarah cannot resist the Doctor's plea that she accompany him one more time. While Sarah appears quite invulnerable, she really does need a bit of protection now and then.

HARRY SULLIVAN

Young, handsome, with blue eyes and curly hair, Harry Sullivan has a medical degree and is a first-class boxer. He's a pretty conventional guy, but he does have an adventurous streak. That streak made him join up with UNIT, the United Nations Intelligence Taskforce created to protect the Planet Earth from extraterrestrial invasion.

#9

AND THE ANDROID INVASION
by Terrance Dicks

PINNACLE BOOKS   •   **NEW YORK**

This is a work of fiction. All the characters and events portrayed in this book are fictional, and any resemblance to real people or incidents is purely coincidental.

DOCTOR WHO AND THE ANDROID INVASION (#9)

Text of book copyright © 1978 by Terrance Dicks
"Doctor Who" series copyright © 1977 by the
British Broadcasting Corporation
Introduction copyright © 1980 by Harlan Ellison

All rights reserved, including the right to reproduce this book or portions thereof in any form.

A Pinnacle Books edition, published by special arrangement with W. H. Allen & Co. Ltd.
First published in Great Britain.

First printing, January 1980
Second printing, May 1981

ISBN: 0-523-41619-9

Cover illustration by David Mann

Printed in the United States of America

PINNACLE BOOKS, INC.
1430 Broadway
New York, New York 10018

Contents

Introducing *DOCTOR WHO*
amenities performed by
HARLAN ELLISON

They could not have been more offended, confused, enraged and startled. . . . There was a moment of stunned silence . . . and then an eruption of angry voices from all over the fifteen-hundred-person audience. The kids in their Luke Skywalker pajamas (cobbled up from older brother's castoff karate *gi*) and the retarded adults spot-welded into their Darth Vader fright-masks howled with fury. But I stood my ground, there on the lecture platform at the World Science Fiction Convention, and I repeated the heretical words that had sent them into animal hysterics:

"*Star Wars* is adolescent nonsense; *Close Encounters* is obscurantist drivel; 'Star Trek' can turn your brains to purée of bat guano; and the greatest science fiction series of all time is *Doctor Who*! And I'll take you all on, one-by-one or all in a bunch to back it up!"

Auditorium monitors moved in, truncheons ready to club down anyone foolish enough to try jumping the lecture platform; and finally there was relative silence. And I heard scattered voices screaming from the back of the room, "Who?" And I said, "Yes. Who!"

(It was like that old Abbott and Costello routine: Who's on first? No, Who's on third; What's on first.)

After a while we got it all sorted out and they understood that when I said Who I didn't mean *whom*, I meant Who . . . Doctor Who . . . the most famous science fiction character on British television. The renegade Time Lord, the far traveler through Time and Space, the sword of justice from the planet Gallifrey, the scourge of villains and monsters the galaxy over.

The one and only, the incomparable, the bemusing and bewildering Doctor Who, the humanistic defender of Good and Truth whose exploits put to shame those of Kimball Kinnison, Captain Future and pantywaist nerds like Han Solo and Luke Skywalker.

My hero! Doctor Who!

For the American reading (and television-viewing) audience (and in this sole, isolated case I hope they're one and the same) *Doctor Who* is a new factor in the equation of fantastic literature. Since 1963 the Doctor and his exploits have been a consistent element of British culture. But we're only now being treated to the wonderful universes of Who here in the States. For those of us who were exposed to both the TV series on BBC and the long series of *Doctor Who* novels published in Great Britain, the time of solitary proselytizing is at an end. All we need to do now is thrust a Who novel into the hands of the unknowledgeable, or drag the unwary to a TV set and turn it on as the good Doctor goes through his paces. That's all it takes. Try this book and you'll understand.

I envy you your first exposure to this amazing conceit. And I wish for you the same delight I felt when Michael Moorcock, the finest fantasist in the English-speaking world, sat me down in front of his set in London, turned on the telly, and said, "Now be quiet and just watch."

That was in 1975. And I've been hooked on "Doctor Who" ever since. Understand: I despise television (having written it for sixteen years) and I spend much of my time urging people to bash in their picture tubes with Louisville Sluggers, to free themselves of the monster of the coaxial cable. And so, you must perceive that I speak of something utterly extraordinary and marvelous when I suggest you watch the "Doctor Who" series in whatever syndicated slot your local station has scheduled it. You must recognize that I risk all credibility for future exhortations by telling you *this* TV viewing will not harm you . . . will, in fact, delight and uplift you, stretch your imagination, tickle your risibilities, flinch your intellect of all lesser visual sf affections, improve your disposition and clean up your zits. What I'm saying here, case you're a *yotz* who needs things codified simply and directly, is that "Doctor Who" is the apex, the pinnacle, the tops, the Louvre Museum, the Coliseum, and other etcetera.

Now to give you a few basic facts about the Doctor, to brighten your path through this nifty series of lunatic novels.

He is a Time Lord: one of that immensely wise and powerful super-race of alien beings who, for centuries unnumbered, have watched and studied all of Time and Space with intellects (as H.G. Wells put it) vast and cool and unsympathetic. Their philosophy was never to interfere in the affairs of alien races, merely to watch and wait.

But one of their number, known only as the Doctor, found such inaction anathema. As he studied the interplay of great forces in the cosmos, the endless wars and invasions, the entropic conflict between Good and Evil, the rights and lives of a thousand alien life forms debased and brutalized, the wrongs left unrighted . . . he was overcome by the compulsion *to act*! He was a renegade, a misfit in the name of justice.

And so he stole a TARDIS and fled.

Ah, yes. The TARDIS. That most marvelous device for spanning the Time-lines and traversing all of known/unknown Space. The name is an acronym for Time And Relative Dimensions In Space. Marvelous! An amazing machine that can change shape to fit in with any locale in which it materializes. But the TARDIS stolen from his fellow Time Lords by the Doctor was in for repairs. And so it was frozen in the shape of its first appearance: a British police call box. Those of you who have been to England may have seen such call boxes. (There are very few of them extant currently, because the London "bobbies" now have two-way radio in their patrol cars; but before the advent of that communication system the tall, dark blue street call box—something like our old-fashioned wooden phone booth—was a familiar sight in the streets of London. If a police officer needed assistance he could call in directly from such a box, and if the station house wanted to get in touch with a copper they could turn on the big blue light atop the box and its flashing would attract a "bobby.")

Further wonder: the outward size of the TARDIS does not reveal its relative size *inside*. The size of a phone booth outwardly, it is enormous within, holding many sections filled with the Doctor's super-scientific equipment.

Unfortunately, the stolen TARDIS needed more repairs than just the fixing of its shape-changing capabilities. Its steering mechanism was also wonky, and so the Doctor could never be certain that the coordinates he set for time and place of materializing would be correct. He might set course for the planet Karn . . . and wind up in Victorian London. He might wish to relax at an intergalactic pleasure resort . . . and pop into existence in Antarctica. He might lay in a course for the deadly gold mines of Voga . . . and appear in Renaissance Italy.

It makes for a chancy existence, but the Doctor takes it all unflinchingly. As do his attractive female traveling companions, whose liaisons with the Doctor are never sufficiently explicated for those of us with a nasty, suspicious turn of mind.

The Doctor *looks* human and, apart from his quirky way of thinking, even *acts* human most of the time. But he is a Time Lord, not a mere mortal. He has two hearts, a stable body temperature of 60°, and—not to stun you too much—he's approximately 750 years old. Or at least he was that age when the first of the 43 *Doctor Who* novels was written. God (or Time Lords) only knows how old he is now!

Only slightly less popular than the good Doctor himself are his arch-foes and the distressing alien monsters he battles through the pages of these wild books and in phosphor-dot reality on your TV screens. They seem endless in their variety: the Vardans, the Oracle, Fendahl, the virus swarm of the Purpose, The Master, the Tong of the Black Scorpion, the evil brain of Morbius, the mysterious energy force known as the Mandragora Helix, the android clone Kraals, the Zygons, the Cybermen, the Ice Warriors, the Autons, the spore beast called the Krynoid and—most deadly and menacing of them all—the robot threat of the Daleks.

Created by mad Davros, the great Kaled scientist, the pepper-pot-shaped Daleks made such an impression in England when they were first introduced into the series that they became a cultural artifact almost immediately. Movies have been made about them, toys have been manufactured of Daleks, coloring books, Dalek candies, soaps, slippers, Easter eggs and even special Dalek fireworks. They rival the Doctor for the attention of a fascinated audience and they have been brought back again and again during the fourteen years the series has perpetuated itself on BBC television; and their shiveringly pleasurable manifestations have not been confined just to England and America. Doctor Who and the Daleks have millions of rabid fans in over thirty countries around the world.

Like the three fictional characters *every* nation knows—Sherlock Holmes, Tarzan and Superman— Doctor Who seems to have a universal appeal.

Let me conclude this paean of praise with these thoughts: hating *Star Wars* and "Star Trek" is not a difficult chore for me. I recoil from that sophomoric species of creation that excuses its simplistic cliche structure and homage to the transitory (as does *Star Wars*) as violently as I do from that which sententiously purports to be deep and intellectual when it is, in fact, superficial self-conscious twaddle (as does "Star Trek"). This is not to say that I am an ivory tower intellect whose doubledome can only support Proust or Descartes. When I was a little kid, and was reading everything I could lay hands on, I read the classics with joy, but enjoyed equally those works I've come to think of as "elegant trash": the Edgar Rice Burroughs novels, The Shadow, Doc Savage, Conan, comic books and Uncle Wiggly. They taught me a great deal of what I know about courage and truth and ethics in the world.

To that list I add *Doctor Who*. His adventures are sunk to the hips in humanism, decency, solid adventure and simple good reading. They are not classics, make no mistake. They can never touch the illuminative level of Dickens or Mark Twain or Kafka. But they are solid entertainment based on an understanding of Good and Evil in the world. They say to us, "You, too, can be Doctor Who. You, like the good Doctor, can stand up for that which is bright and bold and true. You can shape the world, if you'll only go and try."

And they do it in the form of *all* great literature . . . the cracking good, well-plotted adventure yarn. They are direct lineal heirs to the adventures of Rider Haggard and Talbot Mundy, of H.G. Wells and Jules Verne, of Mary Shelley and Ray Bradbury. They are worth your time.

And if you give yourself up to the Doctor's winsome ways, he will take substance and reality in your imagination. For that reason, for the inestimable goodness and delight in every *Doctor Who* adventure, for the benefits he proffers, I lend my name and my urging to read and watch him.

I don't think you'll do less than thank me for shoving you down with this book in your hands, and telling you . . . here's Who. Meet the Doctor.

The pleasure is all mine. And all yours, kiddo.

HARLAN ELLISON
Los Angeles

DR. WHO AND THE
ANDROID INVASION

1

Strange Arrival

A soldier was marching through the forest. He wore the uniform of a corporal in the British Army. His buttons gleamed in the sunlight, his boots shone a glossy black, his trousers were sharply creased and his beret was set at the regulation angle. The rifle on his shoulder was clean, bright, and slightly oiled.

He crossed the forest clearing in a dead straight line, the handsome young face set in an expressionless mask, eyes staring blankly ahead. But a heavy, dragging limp in his loft leg marred the military precision of his pace, that and a spasmodic clenching and unclenching of his left hand.

Although he avoided the trees, lesser obstacles didn't seem to register. A patch of brambles barred his path and he smashed through them like a tank. A thorn ripped a jagged tear down the right side of his face but the soldier didn't seem to notice. He moved on through the forest with his odd, limping march, like a clockwork toy that someone had wound up and sent marching blindly forwards. A clockwork toy that wasn't quite working properly. He reached a dense clump of bushes on the far side of the clearing and came to a sudden jerky halt, standing motionless at attention, as still as one of the trees.

Minutes later, a strange sound disturbed the peace of the forest, a kind of wheezing, groaning noise. An old blue police callbox materialized out of nowhere, standing four-square and solid in the little clearing. The door opened and a very tall man stepped out. He had wide staring eyes and a tangle of curly hair and he wore an assortment of loose-fitting tweedy, vaguely Bohemian garments topped off with a battered broad-brimmed soft hat and an incredibly long scarf.

A slender dark-haired girl followed him out of the police callbox. She wore casual, late twentieth-century clothes, with a brightly-colored scarf at her throat. She looked searchingly at the forest around her and drew a deep, satisfied breath. "There you are, Doctor, I told you we'd reached Earth. Just sniff. That's real air, that is."

"Possibly, Sarah. Possibly."

Sarah looked uneasily at him. She had been the Doctor's companion through two lives and a number of fantastic adventures, journeying through Time and Space in his TARDIS. By now she was looking forward to returning home—and she didn't even want to consider the possibility that something had gone wrong with the TARDIS's ever-erratic steering mechanism. "What do you mean—possibly?"

"The coordinates were set for Earth, but the linear calculator's been a little unreliable recently. It may just possibly have——"

"Gone up the creek again?" Sarah shook her head. "No, this is Earth all right!" She took another deep breath. "I love that fresh smell you get just after rain."

The Doctor sniffed. "Yes, it does have that characteristic smell of wet earth . . . which is rather strange, when you look at the ground."

"What about it?"

The Doctor stooped and picked up a handful of soil. It was dry and crumbly, trickling away between his fingers. "It's bone dry. There hasn't been any rain here for weeks." He fished a small compass-like device from one of his pockets and studied the dial. The needle oscillated wildly for a moment, then swung firmly to the top of its scale. "Now what could be causing that?"

"Causing what?"

"There's some enormous energy source, not very far away." The Doctor moved over to a tree and began studying it suspiciously.

Sarah followed him. "You don't really think there's been some mistake, do you? I mean we are on Earth?"

"Well, unless someone's started exporting

3

acorns. English oaks don't grow anywhere else in the galaxy, as far as I know."

Sarah felt reassured. "Come on, Doctor, let's try and find out where we are."

As they moved away, they passed the clump of bushes which was hiding the soldier. He was still standing there, perfectly motionless, eyes staring fixedly ahead, and they went by without seeing him. Soon after they'd gone, he resumed his jerky march, as if someone had wound him up and set him going again.

The Doctor and Sarah moved on through the silent forest, Sarah staring uneasily around her. Although things looked normal, somehow they didn't feel normal. Just as they reached another clearing, Sarah stopped, putting a hand on the Doctor's arm. "Wait a minute."

"What is it?"

"I heard something moving—over there."

Four figures came out of the trees. They wore white, high-necked overalls, and strange-looking helmets with dark visors that hid their faces. They looked vaguely like racing drivers or mechanics, thought Sarah. But what were four racing drivers doing in the middle of a wood?

"Oh, good!" said the Doctor cheerfully. "Now we can find out where we are."

"No, wait, I don't like the look of them . . ."

But the Doctor had already stepped out into the clearing. "Hullo, there! I wonder if you could tell us exactly where we are?"

4

The four white-clad mechanics stopped. Then, moving as one man, they raised their right arms in front of them, fingers pointed accusingly at the Doctor.

The Doctor stared hard at those pointing fingers and realized they ended in open tubes—like gun-muzzles. He flung himself down just as the fingers spat fire.

Scrambling to his feet, the Doctor ran back into the shelter of the trees. "Not a very friendly welcome home! We'd better get away from here."

They ran through the trees, shots whizzing close to their heads.

The four mechanics lowered their arms and turned to face each other. They stood motionless, for a moment in silent conference. Then they split up. Two of them turned and went back the way they had come. The two others began following the Doctor and Sarah through the woods.

Sarah ran blindly on, the Doctor close behind her. The woods thinned out, and she saw that a tall thin hedge bordered the edge of the forest, barring their way. Sarah turned and got a glimpse of white overalls moving through the trees behind them. Frantically, she forced her way through the hedge, bursting through to the other side—then the ground disappeared from beneath her feet.

The Doctor shot through the hedge behind her and threw himself forward, grabbing Sarah's wrist as she disappeared from sight. He dropped face down, bracing himself to take the shock of her weight.

Sarah found herself dangling in empty space, supported only by the Doctor's grip. She looked down and saw the rocky ground horribly far below her. Slowly the Doctor began hauling her back to safety.

Sarah scrambled back over the cliff edge, and sat gasping for breath. They were on the edge of a deep quarry which ran parallel with the edge of the woods. Apparently disused, it formed a deep, narrow valley, the sides overgrown with bushes and scrubby grass. Sarah looked at the Doctor. "Thanks. I should have looked before I leaped!"

The Doctor grinned. "My pleasure. After all, I couldn't leave you hanging around, could I?"

Sarah groaned, thinking that nothing seemed to quell the Doctor's taste for terrible jokes. She got shakily to her feet. The Doctor indicated a steep path winding its way down to the quarry floor. "Let's try that way, shall we? Not so quick as your method, but a lot safer."

He was about to lead the way when he saw movement in the bushes some way away. At first he thought the mechanics had caught up with them, and prepared to run. But the figure that emerged wore not white, but khaki—the uniform of a corporal in the British Army. It came forward in a jerky, limping march, making straight for the sheer drop at the quarry's edge.

"Hey, look out!" yelled the Doctor. "Stop! Stay where you are!"

The soldier didn't seem to hear him. Face blank, eyes staring, he marched steadily forward.

"Stop!" yelled Sarah. "Look out, you'll fall." They began running along the edge of the quarry. But the distance between them and the soldier was greater than that between the soldier and the quarry edge, and they had no chance of reaching him in time. He marched jerkily over the edge and hurtled down to the ground.

Sarah stared down at the spreadeagled body, so far below that it looked like a broken doll. "Why didn't he stop, Doctor? He must have heard us."

The Doctor was already heading for the path. "It's probably too late but we'd better get down to him. Come on."

They scrambled down the path and across the rocky ground to the crumpled body. It was sprawled face down, huddled like an old sack. To Sarah's relief there didn't seem to be any blood.

The Doctor shook his head. "The fall must have killed him instantly." He began looking through the pockets in the army uniform.

Sarah still couldn't believe what she'd just

7

seen. "He went over that cliff as if he was sleep walking." She shuddered at the memory. "Found anything?"

The Doctor held out a handful of coins. "Take a look at these."

"What about them?"

"They're all mint-fresh. No scratches, no tarnish. There's something else too." He looked expectantly at her.

Sarah examined the coins one by one. "They look all right to me. No, wait a minute. They've all got the same date!"

"Exactly. And what are the odds against someone getting a whole pocketful of small change all of the same date?"

"I just don't understand it . . ."

The Doctor plunged his hands into his pockets and began pacing about the quarry, rather like a bloodhound questing for a lost scent. "Neither do I—yet. But . . ."

"But what?"

"What indeed," said the Doctor absently. His attention had been caught by an oddly-shaped rock on the far side of the quarry and he went to examine it.

Sarah followed him. The rock, if it was a rock, was about eight feet long, and it seemed to have split into two identically shaped hollow halves, rather like a giant pea pod. Put together they would have made a long, hollow object, shaped, thought Sarah uneasily, rather like a lumpy coffin. The outer surface was made of charred, pitted rock, rather like a meteorite, The Doctor ran his hand along the hollow interior. It was lined with some dark, soft mossy material that felt rather like foam rubber.

Sarah watched him impatiently. "Come on, Doctor, time we were moving on."

"Wait a moment, this is fascinating . . ."

"It's just an old canister. People are always dumping rubbish in disused quarries."

"Thing is, I've seen something like this before. My memory's getting terrible these days."

"It certainly is. You seem to have forgotten we were being shot at just a few minutes ago."

As if to reinforce Sarah's words a bullet spanged off a nearby rock.

The Doctor looked up. Two white-clad figures had appeared on the rim of the quarry. "We seem to have annoyed them again, don't we? Come on!"

They ran along the quarry and out of a broken gate at the far end. Bullets buzzed angrily around them like giant bees, but none seemed to be coming very close. Perhaps their attackers had only got short-range fingers, thought Sarah hysterically.

The gate led into a muddy country lane between high hedges, and the lane in turn joined onto a country road. They rounded a bend and there before them lay an extremely pretty country village. They slowed their pace, and soon the road widened and became the village's main street. They saw a traditional village

9

green complete with war memorial, thatched cottages, old-fashioned shops, and an appropriately rustic-looking village inn. It all looked like the cover photograph on a "Holidays in Britain" travel brochure. The fact that there wasn't a soul in sight added to the growing feeling of unreality.

"Well, well," said the Doctor cheerfully. "Civilization at last!" He surveyed the picturesque scene. "Something familiar about all this . . . I think I've been through here before."

Sarah fell into step beside him, gazing curiously about her. As they walked through the village she too felt a growing sense of familiarity. "Devesham!" she said suddenly.

"You know this village?"

"I came here on a story a couple of years ago."

"Is it always this quiet?"

Sarah looked round. They were in the center of the village by now, but there wasn't a single human being to be seen. "No, it isn't. It's usually a bustling little place."

"Hello!" yelled the Doctor suddenly. "Anyone about?" Silence. His voice echoed across the empty village green, but no one answered.

The village of Devesham lay peacefully in the morning sunlight—completely deserted.

2

Village of Terror

"Let's try the village inn," said the Doctor hopefully. "Bound to be someone in there."

He led the way to the inn, pushed open the door, and stopped, looking round in astonishment.

They were in a typical English country pub. A long mahogany bar-counter ran across the rear of the room. There were gleaming beer-pumps, and an array of bottles on shelves behind the bar. There were oak booths against the walls, and a scattering of chairs and tables. A mixed assortment of drinks stood on the tables, half-finished pints of ale, glasses of lager, the occasional glass of whiskey or gin. There was sawdust on the floor, horse-brasses gleaming on the walls, a dartboard, all the ingredients of a picturesque country pub. Everything but people. Like the village outside, the place was deserted.

The Doctor marched up to the bar. "Landlord?" There was no reply.

"Anybody here?" shouted Sarah. Silence.

11

The Doctor looked round the empty bar. "What's this pub called?"

"The Fleur de Lys."

"They ought to re-name it 'The Marie Celeste'!"

"It's crazy. A village full of people can't just disappear."

The Doctor went round behind the bar and opened the old-fashioned till. "Here we are again . . ."

"What?"

He flung a handful of coins on the bar. "Freshly-minted money. Brand-new coins—and all the same year. Sarah . . . you said you came down here on a story. What story?"

"Something about a missing astronaut. It was at that new Space Research Center. It's just outside the village."

The Doctor nodded. "Yes, I know the place— I actually went there once with the Brigadier." He rubbed his chin. "You know, that could explain a lot. If we landed in a prohibited area those people who shot at us could have been some kind of guards."

"With built-in finger guns? Trespassers are prosecuted in England, Doctor—not shot. And they weren't dressed like guards."

The Doctor shrugged. "Protective clothing, against some kind of radioactivity. I detected an energy-source, remember . . . the soldier who walked over the cliff could have been affected by it."

"Radiation sickness?"

"Something of the kind, yes."

"And this village?"

"Evacuated."

Sarah waved towards the unfinished drinks on the tables all around them. "It must have been done in a pretty big hurry."

"There may have been some kind of emergency. A sudden radiation leakage . . ."

"That's great! And we've been walking around in the middle of it like a couple of great idiots!" She nodded towards the coins on the bar. "And what about all this new money?"

"Anti-contamination procedure, perhaps. Money changes hands. They might have thought it necessary to bring in completely clean currency."

"Are you serious, Doctor?"

The Doctor shrugged. "I'm just trying to build a theory that fits all the facts as we know them. It's only a guess, mind you . . ."

"Well, it's a pretty nasty one." Sarah heard a noice and looked out of the window. "Hey, Doctor, look! The village isn't deserted any more."

The Doctor came to join her. Four white-overalled figures were moving down the center of the street, a fifth, uniformed figure walking just behind them. As the little group moved nearer, the fifth figure came into view. Sarah gasped. "No . . . it can't be . . . it *can't*!"

The fifth man wore the uniform of a corporal in the British Army. It was the soldier they'd

13

seen in the woods a little earlier. The one who'd marched straight over the edge of a cliff.

Sarah stared unbelievingly at him. There was no mark on his face, no spasmodic clenching of the hands, no trace of a limp, as he marched along the empty street. He was a dead man walking, apparently none the worse for a fall that should have shattered every bone in his body.

"He was *dead*," whispered Sarah. "We saw him . . ." She backed away from the window, and caught the edge of a table. A glass crashed to the floor.

The little group outside suddenly paused, their heads swinging round in uncanny unison.

"They heard me," whispered Sarah.

The Doctor shook his head. "No, I don't think so. Look."

An army truck was trundling slowly along the high street with about two dozen people in the back. There were both men and women, some young, some middle-aged. They sat bolt-upright on hard wooden benches, staring straight ahead of them. They looked like shop-window dummies, thought Sarah, or a load of wax figures being taken to the museum. The truck came to a halt outside the pub. For a second nobody moved. Then, as if obeying some secret signal, they all rose, climbing stiffly down from the truck. Once on the ground they scattered, most of them heading for the shops and houses along

14

the high street. About a dozen of the men stayed together in a group. Still moving with that frightening, silent unanimity, they began marching towards the pub.

Sarah pointed. "That man in front, the one in the checkered sports jacket. That's Mr. Morgan, the landlord."

The Doctor was already looking for a place to hide. Not behind the bar, someone would be bound to go through there . . . He spotted a little door in the wall, just beside the bar flap. Seizing Sarah's arm he hurried her towards it.

They found themselves in a tiny storeroom, not much bigger than a cupboard. It was stacked high with empty beer crates and cracker tins. A second door opened on to a rear corridor. The Doctor closed the door to the bar, leaving a crack so they could see into the room.

The front door opened, and a group of men came in. The mysteriously revived soldier came in with them. As if following some prearranged plan, each man moved swiftly to a specific position, some standing against the bar, others sitting at the tables. Morgan went behind the bar and stood with his hand resting on a beer-pump. The Corporal leaned on the bar in front of him.

When everyone was in position, the scene froze. The men stood quite still staring ahead of them. They looked like people posing for one of those old-fashioned photographers, thought

Sarah, in the days when you had to stand perfectly still for several minutes. Or like actors, waiting for their cue. So complete was the silence that Sarah could hear a faint whirring, clicking noise, the sound a clock makes just before it strikes. She looked at the big old-fashioned clock. It was a few seconds before twelve o'clock. Suddenly the big hand jerked and the first chime rang out.

Immediately the bar came to life. Morgan reached for a glass, pulled back the beer handle, and served a pint of beer to the waiting Corporal. All over the room men reached for their glasses. There was a low rumble of conversation. A couple of men started playing darts, and at the corner table two others got on with their game of dominoes. Everything was utterly, shatteringly normal.

The Doctor studied the scene for a moment, then pulled the storeroom door closed. "Extraordinary. Quite extraordinary."

"What's the matter with them all?" whispered Sarah.

"I don't know—but I intend to find out."

"How?"

"The Space Research Station. I think UNIT are responsible for security there. Maybe they'll have some answers."

(UNIT was the United Nations Intelligence Taskforce, to which the Doctor was loosely attached as Scientific Adviser.)

"And what do I do?"

"Keep an eye on things here. You'll be all right."

"I've heard that one before!"

The Doctor slipped the TARDIS key-chain from around his neck, and handed it to Sarah. "Can you find your way back to the TARDIS?"

"Of course I can."

"If anything goes wrong, meet me there." He opened the rear door, slipped out into the corridor and disappeared.

"Typical," thought Sarah bitterly. "Goes off and leaves me to it just when things are getting tricky." What was she supposed to do now? "Keep an eye on things" was a pretty vague instruction.

In the bar everyone was still chatting amiably. The Corporal finished his pint, and pushed his mug across the bar for another one. As Morgan began refilling it, the Corporal glanced idly round the bar—and caught sight of the handle of the storeroom door. It was moving, and as he watched, the door opened the merest crack.

He stepped swiftly across the bar, caught hold of the handle and jerked the door fully open. Sarah was revealed, standing on the threshold. All conversation cut off immediately, and everyone in the bar swung round to look at her.

Sarah decided that since she'd been discovered she might as well try to bluff her way through. She stepped bravely into the bar. "Afternoon everyone!" She looked up at the clock.

"Well, just about afternoon anyway." She moved over to the bar. "Hullo, Mr. Morgan. You remember me, don't you? Sarah Jane Smith. I'm a journalist. I came here on a story a couple of years ago."

Morgan didn't say anything. No one said anything. They just stood silently looking at her. There was a kind of threat in the silence, and Sarah felt a growing sensation of unease. "Well, somebody say something."

It was the Corporal who spoke at last. "Who sent you here? What do you want? How did you get here?"

Sarah didn't want to get into involved explanations about the TARDIS. "I walked."

"Where have you come from? Why are you here?"

The succession of questions began to fray Sarah's nerves. She turned angrily to Morgan. "Do you let him grill all your customers like this? Just because he's in the Army . . ."

Morgan said heavily, "We don't have strangers here." He spoke as if repeating some kind of universally accepted law.

"That ridiculous. This place is always full of tourists."

The Corporal began moving purposefully towards Sarah, reaching out as if to take her arm. As Sarah backed away Morgan said, "Corporal Adams, wait. She may be part of the test."

Adams nodded, and stepped back.

Sarah was beginning to feel trapped in some endless nightmare. "Test? What test?"

Adams looked at Morgan. "She does not know."

"Look, what's going on here?" demanded Sarah. "What don't I know?"

"Perhaps they would not have told her," said Morgan slowly. He turned back to Sarah. "I think you'd better go, miss."

"Why?"

"It might be best."

Sarah looked round the circle of blank, silent faces. "Look, if there's some sort of trouble here, why not tell me about it? Perhaps I can help."

No one spoke. Sarah shrugged and moved towards the door. "Well, I intend to find out anyway." She looked at Corporal Adams, unable to resist a parting shot. "As for you, I'm sure you shouldn't be drinking, so soon after breaking your neck!" With that, Sarah marched out of the bar.

For a moment the silent figures stared after her. Then they jerked into life, and the babble of conversation struck up again. Morgan filled Corporal Adam's mug and pushed it across the bar. Adams paid for his beer, and took an appreciative swig. Just a normal morning in an English country pub.

* * *

Sarah marched indignantly down the village street, wondering what everyone was playing at. She decided to follow the Doctor to the Space Research Center and insist on some explanation. By now her journalist's instincts were fully roused. Something very odd was happening in this picturesque little village, and there had to be a story in it.

As she came level with the parked army truck, a white-clad figure stepped out from behind it. Coming forward, it raised the dark visor on its helmet. Sarah stopped, looking curiously at its face. But there *was* no face—the space beneath the visor was dark and empty. The thing was headless, yet it was stalking towards her. In blind terror, Sarah turned and ran.

3

The Watcher

The Doctor walked confidently up to the main
gate of the Space Research Center. It was a
vast, sprawling, ultra-modern building, all glass
and concrete. A forest of weirdly shaped aerials
sprouted from its roof, which was dominated by
a huge saucer-shaped radar dish. The Center
had its own rocket landing field close by, and
the whole complex was enclosed by a high wall.

Usually the main gate was almost excessively
well-guarded. It was impossible to get inside
without much flashing of top-secret passes, and
the Doctor was quite prepared to have to talk
his way in. But to his astonishment he found the
main gates standing open, with no sentry in
sight. The whole place seemed deserted. Puzzled, the Doctor went up the front steps and
through the main doors.

The scanner room lay in the very heart of the
Space Research Center. It was packed with
complex instruments which monitored the sur-

rounding countryside and reached far out into deep space.

A white-coated figure was hunched over a central control console, headphones over his ears. Grierson was chief technician at the Center, a burly figure who looked more like an engineer than a scientist. He was listening intently, a worried frown on his face. After a moment he took off the earphones and straightened up. He hesitated for a moment, then his finger stabbed at a button. Immediately, the face of a man in his forties appeared on a monitor screen. He looked worn and haggard and he wore a black patch over his left eye. "Well, what is it now, Grierson? You know I'm busy."

"Sorry to disturb you, Commander Crayford. But I've got a strange audio response on the ground scanner. Some kind of energy-source."

The monitor went dark, and a few minutes later Crayford hurried in. He wore the simple military-style uniform of the newly created Space Service. "All right, let's have a listen."

Grierson handed him the headphones. "I reckon it's a power-frequency of some kind, sir."

Crayford listened for a moment, then took off the headset. "Turn it to maximum." A steady, resonant pinging sound came through a nearby loudspeaker. "Any movement?"

"No,sir, it's quite stationary."

Crayford studied a display panel. "Seems to be about a mile away. When was the last scan?"

"About three hours ago, sir. It was negative then."

Gently Crayford rubbed his eye-patch. "Some kind of machine . . ."

"It must be a spacecraft, sir. Come down since the last scan."

Crayford shook his head. "The detectors would have picked it up."

"If it is a spacecraft, it could have its own jamming equipment."

Crayford switched off the speaker. "A spacecraft . . . No, it's just not possible." But his tone was less positive now.

Encouraged, Grierson said, "We've never picked up anything like it before, sir. It's *got* to be something external. That's why I thought I'd better call you."

"It may be some kind of test," said Crayford thoughtfully. "Something they've arranged without telling me, just to keep us on our toes. Can you fix its precise position?"

"Not from here, sir. We'd have to send out a mobile scanner and take a cross-bearing."

Crayford considered. "No need for that yet. I'll report it. There may be some perfectly simple explanation."

Grierson returned to his control console. "Very good, sir."

With a last worried look at the instrument panel, Crayford hurried away.

❊   ❊   ❊

23

The Doctor came to a door with a notice on it. "Inner Security Area. No Entry Without Proper Authority. All Passes Must Be Shown." Unhesitatingly, the Doctor flung open the door—and found himself facing an armed sentry standing rigidly to attention.

"Hullo there," said the Doctor. "Where can I find your Commanding Officer?"

The soldier said nothing. Rifle on shoulder, trousers creased, boots gleaming, he stood rigidly to attention like one of the guards outside Buckingham Palace, forbidden to react, whatever the tourists say or do. The Doctor stared into the man's face. It was completely immobile, the eyes glazed. Somehow the sentry looked—switched off. The Doctor frowned. "Well, I'll tell you what, perhaps I needn't bother you. I'll just go and find him myself." The Doctor moved away. Slowly, very slowly, the sentry turned his head to look after him.

Sarah had run clear out of the village, and was back in the shelter of the woods. Too tired to run further, she hurried on as quickly as she could, heading for the clearing where they'd left the TARDIS. She reached it at last, and leaned against its comforting blue bulk, gasping for breath. Whatever was going on in this sinister place Sarah wanted nothing more to do with it. She was going to wait in the TARDIS until the Doctor turned up and took her to safety. Or more likely, took her somewhere even more dangerous, thought Sarah gloomily. Still for the moment at least she was safe. She slipped the TARDIS key from around her neck and turned it in the lock. She was about to open the door when something caught her eye. Close to the TARDIS, half-sunk in the soft earth of the forest, lay one of the strange long, coffin-shaped rocks, like the one they'd seen in the quarry. But this one was still intact. Sarah hesitated, but her curiosity was too strong for her. She went over to the canister and bent to examine it. Like the other, it had a scarred rock-like surface—and it was warm to the touch. Suddenly she heard a familiar groaning, wheezing noise behind her. She spun round and the TARDIS dematerialized before her eyes. "No, Doctor!" she yelled. "Doctor, don't leave me." But the TARDIS was gone.

Sarah stared in amazement at the space where it had stood. "He can't have gone," she thought dazedly. "I just don't believe it." She was certain the Doctor wouldn't just go off and abandon her. But if the doctor wasn't inside, who or what had moved the TARDIS? She rubbed her hand over her eyes, wondering what on earth she should do.

Meanwhile, something was happening to the canister. A seam cracked open all along its length, and the upper half sprang silently open like a lid. A hand flopped out of the gap, catch-

25

ing Sarah on the leg. She screamed and jumped back.

The hand didn't move again, and Sarah studied it cautiously. It was certainly human, and by the looks of it, female. Cautiously she came forward and lifted the canister lid fully open. Lying inside, looking uncannily like a laid-out corpse, was a woman in her fifties. She was neatly and plainly dressed in a simple tweed suit, and looked exactly like the kind of middle-aged lady you'd see shopping in any main street. So, what was she doing in the middle of a wood, lying inside a meteorite?

The woman's eyes flicked open and she stared up at Sarah. Sarah felt she ought to say something, but could only manage a stammered, "Can I help you?"

She bent over the canister, wondering whether to help the woman out or leave her where she was. She touched the woman's shoulder, and two hands shot up and caught her by the throat. Sarah grabbed the woman's wrists and tried to pull her hands away, but despite her age her attacker was tremendously powerful. With a desperate wrench, Sarah pulled free and backed away, gasping.

The woman sat up. Slowly, her eyes fixed unblinkingly on Sarah, she began climbing out of the canister. Sarah found that the problem of what to do next had been solved. For the second time that day she turned and ran for her life.

* * *

Crayford's office was large, spacious, and ultra-modern in design. It had an empty, unused feel, as though no one had moved in yet. Crayford came into the room, and sat down behind the desk. Chin in hands he gazed blankly ahead of him, as if not entirely sure who he was, or what he was doing there. After a moment he began rubbing nervously at the black patch over his left eye.

A voice spoke from a concealed speaker. "Crayford! Crayford, I say!" The voice was deep and throaty, with a kind of gurgle in it. It was not a human voice.

"Crayford jerked upright. "Yes, Styggron?"

"I ordered all units to recharge stations. The order is not being completely observed."

"I'm sorry, Styggron, I don't understand."

"We have detected movement within the complex," growled the alien voice impatiently. "Another unit may have gone random."

"But the Corporal Adams unit has been recovered and repaired—" began Crayford.

"Check and report." There was total arrogance in the alien voice, as if it was inconceivable that its orders should be disobeyed, or even questioned.

Crayford jumped to his feet. "Immediately, Styggron." He hurried from the office.

As he came out into the corridor, he saw a tall figure turning the corner. Immediately,

Crayford ducked back out of sight. He hurried to the desk and snatched a revolver from a drawer, then hid himself behind the half-open office door.

The Doctor came into the office and looked round. He moved over to the desk and began leafing through the pile of papers. Crayford stepped out of hiding. "Keep your hands where I can see them, please."

The Doctor turned round. "Now those are the friendliest words I've heard since I got here."

"Yes, I'm sure. And just how did you get here?"

"Oh, I just dropped in," said the Doctor vaguely. "I do from time to time, you know." He picked up a map from the desk and began studying it with interest.

Crayford took a pace forward and snatched the map from the Doctor's hands, tossing it on the desk. "I can get the truth from you."

"But you're getting it," said the Doctor mildly. "Who are you, by the way?"

"I'm the one holding the gun—and asking the questions."

The Doctor reached out and took a red-braided Army officer's cap from the top of a filing cabinet. "I just wondered. You're in someone else's office. It says Brigadier Lethbridge-Stewart on the door."

"You know the Brigadier?"

"Known him for years. As a matter of fact, I'm his acting unpaid Scientific Adviser."

"The Doctor," said Crayford slowly. "Yes, I've heard about you."

"Good. And you are?"

"Guy Crayford. I'm Senior Astronaut here."

"How do you do?" said the Doctor politely.

He held out his hand, but Crayford stepped back, raising the revolver. "Let's have those hands up, Doctor—if you *are* the Doctor. You could still be an imposter."

The Doctor raised his hands, studying Crayford thoughtfully. "You're very nervous, aren't you? I think something very strange must be going on here."

Crayford frowned. "You've come to that conclusion, have you, Doctor? Interesting. I think we'd better have you taken care of."

"Look," said the Doctor patiently. "I've a suggestion to make. Call the Brigadier and get him to identify me. My arms are beginning to ache."

"Lethbridge-Stewart's away in Geneva. Colonel Faraday's in charge at the moment." Crayford moved behind the desk and touched a button.

"If you're ringing for the butler," said the Doctor hopefully, "I'm very partial to tea and muffins." He moved closer to the desk.

"You'll be held in detention until your identity has been verified," said Crayford curtly.

The Doctor didn't care for being locked up at the best of times, and he was particularly set against being locked up by people he didn't know or trust. He had an uncomfortable feeling that Crayford already knew he was really the Doctor. That was why he wanted to lock him up.

"Detention!" said the Doctor indignantly. "Not detention. I can't bear being detained." With that, he tipped the desk on top of Crayford and shot out of the room.

Crayford fired automatically, but the shots went harmlessly into the ceiling. He began struggling out from under the desk.

The Doctor dashed along the corridor, and saw the soldier who'd come back to life marching towards him, rifle in hand. He turned and ran back the way he'd come—just as Crayford lurched out of his office doorway and took another shot at him. The Doctor ducked down a side corridor. Unfortunately, it was a dead end—but there was a ladder bolted to the wall, and a hatch in the roof. He swarmed up the ladder, shoved open the hatch and climbed through. Adams and Crayford arrived at the end of the little corridor just in time to see his legs disappear.

"Get after him," snapped Crayford. Hampered by his rifle, Adams started to climb the ladder.

The Doctor came out onto the flat roof of one of the long low buildings that made up the complex. He ran to the edge of the roof and looked over—and jumped back as bullets whined about his head. A little group of soldiers stood on the path below, and they seemed to be using him for target practice.

Sarah was climbing the rear wall of the complex when she heard the sound of shooting. Since the TARDIS had disappeared and she didn't fancy going back to the village, she'd decided to go to the Space Research Center and look for some answers there.

She struggled to the top of the high wall, and got a grandstand view of the entire proceedings. She saw the Doctor running along the roof, and the soldiers firing from below. As she watched another soldier appeared through a hatch in the roof and knelt down, rifle at his shoulder, taking aim at the Doctor . . .

The Doctor saw his danger, and dealt with it in the only way possible. There was no cover on the flat roof and at this range the Corporal could scarcely miss. The Doctor ran to the far edge of the roof on the other side from the firing squad below, and took a flying leap into space. He made a soft landing in a flower bed, jumped to his feet and ran along the path— straight into the middle of a group of white-overalled helmeted mechanics who'd appeared round the corner of a building. The mechanics raised their fingers in that strange, pointing gesture. The Doctor remembered the way those fingers could spit bullets, and raised his hands.

The mechanics surrounded him and led him away.

Sarah watched from the top of the wall as the Doctor was led along the path alongside the building. When the Doctor and his captors were far enough away, she jumped down from the wall, and began trailing after them.

The mechanics led the Doctor to the far side of the complex. They took him through a side entrance and down a long corridor lined with metal doors. They opened one apparently at random, thrust him inside, and slammed the door behind. He heard the rattle of bars and bolts, and then footsteps moving away.

The Doctor was in a standard prison-type cell, just a bare metal room furnished only with a built-in bunk. To his utter astonishment, he heard a familiar voice whisper. "Doctor? Are you in there? Can you hear me?"

He went to the cell door and peered through the spy-grille. Sarah was in the corridor. "What on earth are you doing here?" he whispered.

Sarah grinned. "Rescuing you, for a change." She began wrestling with the heavy bolts.

In the wall just behind her a little metal panel slid back. It was about the size of a mail box, and through it two deep-set alien eyes were staring unblinkingly at her. They were the eyes of Styggron, Chief Scientist of the Kraals.

4

Hunted

The bolts drew back at last, and Sarah pulled open the cell door. (Behind her the metal panel slid back into place, and the watching eyes disappeared.) Sarah sensed a flicker of movement and swung round but there was nothing to be seen. The Doctor shot out into the corridor, and saw Sarah peering over her shoulder. "What is it?"

"I thought I saw something. What have you been up to, Doctor?"

"Tell you later," said the Doctor briefly. "Come on, let's get out of here."

Like a spider at the center of its web, Styggron crouched over an instrument console in the secret Kraal control room below the Space Research Center. He touched a control and Crayford appeared on a monitor screen. "Yes, Styggron?"

"I have just observed a second random unit

in the cell area. It has released the first. What has gone wrong?"

"A second unit?"

"These patterns were not programmed," growled Styggron. "Explain!"

"Was this second unit a female?"

"Yes, one of the village section by the looks of her. Check the control directives, a fault must have developed."

"It's not a random unit at all, Styggron—and neither was the first. Something quite extraordinary has happened."

"If they are not random units—then what are they?"

"Space travelers! The male is known as the Doctor. He advises the humans on defense. The female is his companion. They have arrived in the biomagnetron by error."

There was a moment's pause, then the alien voice said suspiciously, "By error? Or by design? If this Doctor advises the humans on defense——" He was interrupted by the howl of the alarm siren.

"The guards have spotted them," said Crayford eagerly.

"After them, Crayford, after them! They must not escape!"

As the sound of the alarm siren died away, a squad of rifle-carrying soldiers came clattering down the corridor and disappeared through the doors at the far end. Once they were gone, a closet door opened, and the Doctor and Sarah slipped cautiously out.

"That was a near one," whispered Sarah. "What on earth did you do?"

"Do?"

"To stir them all up like this. I mean, they seem to be taking you very seriously."

"I didn't do anything. Finding me on the premises was enough to upset Crayford."

Sarah stared at him. "Did you say Crayford?"

The Doctor nodded. "Chap called Guy Crayford. Said he was Senior Astronaut."

"But that's impossible. You remember I told you I came here on a story, about two years ago? That's when Guy Crayford was killed."

"How?"

"It was the first test of the new XK5 scout ship. They sent him out into deep space, then they lost him. The ship just vanished. They thought he must have hit an asteroid or something. Take it from me, Doctor, Guy Crayford is dead."

Crayford sat at his desk, looking up at the tiny monitor lens concealed high in the opposite wall. "I assure you, there is no cause for alarm, Styggron. The complex is being thoroughly searched, section by section. All exits have been covered and the guards have been ordered to shoot on sight."

35

"Countermand that order," said the alien voice. "They must be kept alive for pattern analysis."

"We already have a complete pattern analysis for both the village and the defense complex," protested Crayford.

"Do as I say. The Doctor may have learned of the Kraal plan. He may be here to spy on us. It is essential for us to *know*."

Crayford shook his head. "No, Styggron. While they live they are a danger to all of us. They must be destroyed."

The Doctor and Sarah hurried along yet another corridor. Behind them they could hear distant sounds of pursuit: the clatter of booted feet, shouted orders, the braying of the alarm sirens. For the moment at least, their pursuers seemed to be heading in the wrong direction. The sprawling layout of the research center was working to their advantage.

As they approached a corridor junction, the Doctor paused and held up his hand for silence. Someone was walking up and down not far away. The Doctor glanced round. They were in a stretch of bare corridor, no handy offices or closets to duck into. The Doctor peered cautiously around the corner, then straightened up with a smile on his face. "Well, well, well!" He motioned Sarah forward. The corridor led to a reception area, and a familiar figure stood guarding the doors.

"Small world, isn't it?" said the Doctor delightedly.

Sarah hurried forward. "Hello, Mr. Benton!"

The tall uniformed figure of Company Sergeant-Major Benton swung round to face them, a submachine gun cradled in his arms. But there was no sign of the welcome grin that Sarah had expected. The big soldier's face was cold and hard. The machine-gun swung up to cover them.

Sarah stared unbelievingly at him. Benton was an old friend, a loyal companion in many a dangerous adventure. Now he didn't even seem to recognize them. "Mr. Benton," she called. "It's *us*!"

The machine-gun was trained on them now, rock-steady in Benton's big hands. There was a click as he thumbed back the safety-catch.

"No, Benton," shouted the Doctor. "Don't!"

Styggron wasn't used to opposition, and he didn't care for it. "Enough, Crayford," he roared. "You *shall* do as I say."

Crayford wilted beneath the blast of anger. "Very well." He spoke into his communicator. "All units. The order to kill is cancelled. I repeat. Cancelled!"

* * *

Helplessly the Doctor watched Benton's finger tighten on the trigger. Then, miraculously, the finger relaxed. Benton lowered the gun and stood as if waiting, his face blank.

The Doctor sprang forward, gave Benton a shove that sent him reeling back, grabbed Sarah by the hand and hauled her through the doors.

Benton staggered against the wall, recovered, and ran around the corner to a phone set into the wall. Immediately, the main doors opened again, and the Doctor tiptoed back through them, pulling an astonished Sarah. They ducked down behind the central reception desk, which was big enough to hide them both completely.

Benton was still talking into the phone. "That's right, the entrance to B Block. They've just escaped." Minutes later a squad of armed soldiers came thundering through the main doors. Immediately Benton took charge. "Corporal—with me. We'll alert the other patrols. The rest of you, after them. Spread out!"

Benton and the Corporal hurried off down the corridor, while the rest of the soldiers dashed away. Cautiously the Doctor raised his head.

From somewhere below him a muffled voice said, "Why did we come back? We should have hoofed it while we had the chance. We're bound to be caught now."

The Doctor shook his head, listening as the sounds of pursuit moved away from the building. "On the contrary, we've got them going in the wrong direction. The farther they spread out searching for us, the better our chances of getting away."

They heard the sound of running feet and ducked down. The Doctor risked a quick look and saw yet another squad of soldiers, this time led by Crayford himself. With them was a handsome broad-shouldered young man with curly hair, immaculate in the uniform of a naval lieutenant.

The Doctor heard Crayford say, "Sullivan!"

"Yes, sir?"

"Take a mobile troop, and put a cordon on the perimeter road."

"Very good, sir. I'll get on to it right away."

At the sound of the answering voice, Sarah almost popped up again, but the Doctor's hand held her down. The footsteps moved away, and after a moment the Doctor released his hold. Sarah shot up like a jack-in-the-box. "That was Harry, Doctor!" Harry Sullivan was UNIT's medical officer and another old friend. "What does he think he's up to? He's not even a soldier."

The Doctor grinned. "Well, that should improve our chances a bit."

Baffled, Sarah shook her head. "All our old friends are turning against us . . . hunting for us."

"Led by a dead man," said the Doctor. "Fascinating, isn't it?"

Sarah shivered. "Doctor, what *is* going on here?"

"I think Crayford didn't die in space after all. And when he finally came back to Earth, he wasn't alone. Something came with him. Something that is controlling every human being for miles around."

"Including Harry and Benton." Sarah sighed. "Where to now, Doctor?"

"Back to the village, I think. Somehow we've got to tell London what's going on!"

The Doctor and Sarah dropped down from the perimeter wall, and ran for the shelter of the woods. As the Doctor had hoped, their enemies were widely scattered and hunting in the wrong part of the complex, and they'd managed to get clear of the center unseen.

Once inside the wood, they paused to regain their breath.

"Well, so far so good," said the Doctor optimistically.

"As the man said when he fell off the skyscraper," added Sarah. She looked round the woods. It was gloomy in between the sheltering trees, and uncannily silent. "Have you noticed something, Doctor? There are no birds in these woods."

The Doctor listened. "Well, now that you mention it . . ."

"It's eerie. No birds, no animals of any kind."

From somewhere behind them there came the sound of deep, full-throated baying. "Bloodhounds are animals," said the Doctor grimly. "I think we'd better get a move on."

They hurried on through the forest, but it was difficult to move quickly over the soft leaf-covered ground, and the baying came closer and closer. The Doctor loped ahead, and Sarah did her best to keep up with him. Then her foot caught on a hidden root, and she tripped and fell. The Doctor helped her up. "All right?"

"Yes, I think so."

"Good girl. Come on then." The Doctor ran on, but when Sarah tried to follow, a stab of pain went through her leg. "It's no good, Doctor, I seem to have hurt my ankle."

The savage baying rang out again, much closer now. The Doctor turned back. "Don't worry, Sarah, I'll carry you."

"Oh no you won't," said Sarah determinedly. "I'd just slow you down and then we'd both be caught. You'll have to leave me."

The Doctor thought hard. Unfortunately, Sarah was right. If he tried to carry her over this uneven ground the dogs would be up with them both in no time. He made a quick decision. "Give me your jacket then, Sarah, I'll try to draw them off. You can hide in a tree."

Sarah took off her jacket, and the Doctor lifted her until she could grab a low-lying tree-branch. He boosted her up until she could haul herself higher into the tree and conceal herself

41

amongst the leaves. The Doctor dragged Sarah's jacket across the ground, making a trail leading away from the tree. As he moved away he called, "You stay up there until they've gone by. I'll meet you back at the village inn. If I'm not there in about an hour, head for the TARDIS."

Trailing the jacket, the Doctor disappeared amongst the trees. "Doctor," called Sarah softly. "There's something I forgot to tell you . . ." But the Doctor was already out of earshot, and Sarah didn't dare shout louder in case she alerted their pursuers.

Clinging to the branch, Sarah listened as the barking dogs came nearer and nearer. So much had happened since her rescue of the Doctor . . . now she'd forgotten to tell him the TARDIS had mysteriously disappeared!

5

Captured

Dragging the coat behind him the Doctor ran through the forest at breakneck speed. Anyone who thought the fox actually enjoyed the hunt, should try being chased across country by dogs themselves, he thought grimly.

Despite his speed, the hounds were getting steadily closer. The Doctor ran on. Soon he was out of the shelter of the trees and running across a patch of open country. The ground sloped downwards suddenly. The Doctor bounded to the bottom of the slope and found a huge lake barring his way. He paused for a moment, looking behind him. The country around the lake was bare and open. The barking dogs were very close now, and he'd run straight into his pursuers if he turned back. The lake was broad: if he swam across the soldiers might arrive while he was still in the water, an easy target for their rifles.

The Doctor thought hard. The lake was bordered by several thick clumps of reeds. He plucked a reed and blew thoughtfully through the hollow tube. Quickly he stripped off his coat, and shoes, and bundling them together with Sarah's coat, thrust them into the middle of a nearby bush. He hurried back to the lake.

Not long afterwards a squad of soldiers ran down to the lake. Corporal Adams was in command, and two of the soldiers held huge bloodhounds straining at the leash. The hunters stopped, and looked about them. There was open country all around, the lake lay placid and undisturbed, and there was more open country on the far side. But the Doctor was nowhere in sight.

The baffled dogs cast up and down the bank, looking for a scent, and soon one of them unearthed the bundle of clothing.

Adams turned it over with his foot. "They must have swum across to confuse the scent. Half of you go around that way, and the rest come with me. We'll try to cut them off." The group divided and set off in opposite directions around the lake.

A few minutes after the soldiers moved off, one of the rushes rose from the lake's surface like a submarine periscope. Beneath it was the Doctor, the hollow reed in his mouth. He'd been hiding under the surface, using the reed as a breathing tube.

Wringing out his wet clothes he hurried to the bush, and put on those that were still dry.

* * *

44

Sarah crouched motionless on her high branch while the soldiers and dogs moved beneath her through the forest. After that she waited and waited. Finally her patience ran out, and she climbed carefully down from her tree. Supporting herself on the trunk, she tested her ankle. Luckily it had been bruised rather than sprained, and she found she could walk with only the slightest of limps. Remembering the Doctor's instructions, she set off for the village.

When he found no trace of the Doctor and Sarah on the far side of the lake, Corporal Adams began to suspect his quarry must have doubled back. Quickly he led his men back through the woods. Then as they neared the village, the dogs began to whine and bark, and Adams saw a figure hurrying through the trees. "There she is," he shouted, and the soldiers ran forward.

Sarah heard the noise behind her and tried to run. But her ankle slowed her pace to a stumbling trot, and very soon the soldiers began to close in. She stumbled and fell—and by the time she got to her feet, she was surrounded by armed men. A fist struck her behind the ear and she fell to the ground. The soldiers picked up the limp body and carried it away.

❊ ❊ ❊

Styggron looked up as Crayford's face appeared on his monitor screen. "Well? Report! Report!"

"The girl has been taken, Styggron. The Doctor must be somewhere nearby. Soon we shall have him too."

"No! Locate him, but do not seize him. I have other plans for the Doctor."

The Doctor squelched towards the village, thankful that at least some of his clothes were still dry. Luckily his Time Lord constitution was strongly resistant to colds. He hurried through the outskirts of the village and turned into the main street. As before, it was completely empty. He saw a bus shelter just ahead, a telephone booth standing just beside it. He hurried to the box and was about to go inside when he heard the rumble of a car engine. Quickly he ducked down behind the shelter and waited. An army ambulance drove slowly down the street. Peering from his hiding place, the Doctor saw Corporal Adams at the wheel. As soon as the ambulance was out of sight, the Doctor slipped into the phone booth and picked up the receiver. The phone was dead. He jiggled the receiver-bar, but nothing happened. He slammed down the phone, and headed for the inn.

* * *

Sarah recovered consciousness to a sort of swaying motion Slowly she realized that she was lying down, yet moving at the same time. She opened her eyes and saw corridor walls going past. She was being carried somewhere on a stretcher. But why? Had she been ill? Was she in a hospital? Everything seemed hazy and vague, like that shadowy interval between waking and sleeping. Perhaps she was having a nightmare . . .

She was lifted from the stretcher and placed on a table. An operating table, thought Sarah wildly. She'd been hurt in an accident and now they were going to operate. Strange that there didn't seem to be any pain . . . But of course, they'd given her some kind of drug. That was why everything was so vague. She forced herself to open her eyes, and saw she was in a small circular room which was packed with complicated equipment. Lights flashed before her eyes, and there was a low background of electronic hums and beeps. Sarah frowned. It wasn't like any hospital she'd ever seen . . . The equipment and the room itself were strange. Sarah could distinguish monitor screens and a number of complex instruments, but their shapes were twisted and alien. The place looked like some gloomy underground grotto, a home for trolls and goblins.

A face appeared, hovering above her. It was Harry. Good old Harry Sullivan. Naturally, he'd be there if she'd been hurt. After all, Harry was a doctor himself. Sarah smiled weakly at him, but his face was cold and hard. "It's all right, Miss Smith. Just lie still."

"Harry?" she whispered weakly. Sudden panic swept over her and she started to struggle. But she couldn't move—there were clamps holding her to the table.

A low hypnotic beep began filling Sarah's ears, multicolored lights pulsed steadily in her eyes, and she felt consciousness slipping away . . .

Harry moved away and a moment later another face appeared. It seemed strangely distorted, and Sarah blinked furiously forcing herself to concentrate. As her vision cleared, she gave a gasp of pure horror. The face hovering over her was broad and flat with leathery greenish skin. It was heavily jowled with a squashed pig-like snout, underhung jaw, and enormous ears set flat against a massive skull. Huge eyes glowed in cavernous sockets beneath the jutting brows. The hideous vision loomed larger and larger—then Sarah's head slumped and she slipped into unconsciousness.

The voice of Harry Sullivan said impassively, "She is ready, Styggron."

"Good. Commence the analysis of the brain."

Some time later, Styggron left the disorientation laboratory and returned to his control room. Almost immediately the agitated face of Guy Crayford flashed up on his screen. "The

Doctor has been located in the village. He is being kept under observation as you ordered but . . ."

"Well?"

"I don't like leaving him even this much freedom. He's a dangerous man."

"The Doctor is not a danger to us, Crayford. Not when we can keep him under constant observation."

"But I know his reputation. He's a man of exceptional intelligence. He might discover our entire plan."

"That is why he will make such an excellent subject for experiment," said Styggron arrogantly. "After all, if the Doctor is deceived, we shall know that our programming is perfect."

The Doctor pushed open the door of the inn and looked around. Once again the place was empty. He saw a telephone on the corner of the bar, and he hurried over to it and lifted the receiver. But the phone was dead—just like the one in the village phone booth. The door behind the bar opened suddenly and a burly figure appeared. It was Morgan, the landlord. "Something you want, sir?"

The Doctor replaced the receiver. "Yes, a telephone that works. Yours is out of order."

Morgan leaned on the bar. "Ah, likely it is," he said placidly.

"So is your public phone booth."

49

"There was a gale last night, sir. Brought all the lines down, it did."

The Doctor sighed. "I always told Alexander Bell wires were unreliable."

Morgan looked blankly at him. "Can I get you something to drink, sir?"

The Doctor beamed. "Certainly," he said expansively. "I'll have a pint."

"A pint of what, sir?" asked Morgan patiently.

"A pint of gingerale!"

Morgan reached under the bar and produced a bottle and a glass. As he poured the Doctor's drink, he asked casually, "I suppose you'll be one of them scientists from the Research Center, sir?"

"Yes and no," said the Doctor vaguely. "Or rather, no and yes!" He took a swig of the gingerale. "Get a lot of customers in here, do you?" The Doctor began wandering aimlessly round the bar.

Morgan watched him uneasily. "Not a lot, sir. No one comes here very much. Nothing here, you see. Nothing for strangers in a place like this."

The Doctor lifted a set of darts from the ledge beside the board. "Too quiet, I suppose. Is it always this quiet?"

"On and off, sir. Except for darts club night, of course."

The doctor walked back to the aiming mark, turned, and flung all the darts at once. All three

50

landed quivering in the bullseye. The Doctor strolled back to examine his score. "I see you've got a brand-new board," he said chattily. "This one's never been used."

As he peered curiously at the dartboard, the Doctor's face loomed large on Styggron's monitor screen. Styggron turned triumphantly to the figure at his side. "You see? He is puzzled, suspicious even. But he is not certain."

Styggron's companion was called Chedaki. He had the same flat pig-like features as Styggron, and wore the same tabard-like uniform, with its curious resemblance to a kind of armor. But the insignia on Chedaki's uniform were of different shape and color. Styggron was the Chief Scientist of the Kraal Expedition, while Chedaki was only its military commander.

Not for the first time, scientist and soldier were at loggerheads. "There is no value in this experiment," rumbled Chedaki. "Our strategy is already settled."

"Strategy must be formulated upon knowledge, Chedaki."

"The time for experiments is past, Styggron."

Wearily Styggron shook his massive head at the perpetual narrowness of the military mind. "In the case of Earth, perhaps so. But there are other worlds for the Kraals to conquer. It is important to see that our basic techniques are flawless. And the Doctor is unprogrammed,

Chedaki! A free agent. He can provide a test better than any we can set up ourselves. Crayford!"

Crayford appeared on the screen. "Yes, Styggron?"

"We will now go ahead with the final test."

"Direct communication, Styggron? Is that wise?"

"Yes! Are the preparations complete?"

Crayford said worriedly, "Everything should be ready by now. I'll check." He moved away from the screen.

Chedaki was studying the flow of symbols flashing across a read-out screen. "According to the data drained from the girl, this Doctor has a long association with libertarian causes. His entire history is one of opposition to such conquests as ours. While he is alive he is a threat to us."

Styggron chuckled hoarsely. "The Doctor's history will come to an abrupt end soon. *I* shall end it when I have nothing further to learn from studying him."

"Do not underestimate him, Styggron." Chedaki gestured towards the read-out screen. "The Doctor's record is here. I suggest you study it." He turned and marched angrily from the room.

Stygggron gave a snort of disgust, and turned to the monitor, where the Doctor could be seen sipping his gingerale and chatting idly with the landlord. Styggron brooded over the screen.

"There is no way of escape. What can he do? He is like a wingless fly trapped under my microscope. When his usefulness is ended—I shall crush him." Styggron's great clawed fist smashed down on the control console.

6

The Test

When Crayford reached the disorientation laboratory the operating table was empty. Harry Sullivan was moving about the control room checking instrument readings. Crayford nodded towards the table. "You have finished with the girl?"

"The analysis is complete. We have her memory print and body parameters. They are being coded now."

"See that the girl is well guarded. Styggron wants to run a final test on the Doctor. Inform me as soon as the program is complete."

"Plastic horse brasses," said the Doctor reprovingly. "Ugh!" For some time he had been wandering around the bar examining anything and everything with a curiosty that was somehow both casual and intense at the same time. He looked at Morgan, who was watching him impassively. "I've arranged to meet someone here, Mr. Morgan, but don't let me detain you."

"That's all right," said Morgan heavily.

The Doctor grinned at him. "I can see you're a busy man. Barrels to tap, empties to count, that sort of thing . . ."

"Plenty of time for all that, sir."

"Right then. In that case, I'll have another pint."

"Pint of what, sir?" asked Morgan mechanically.

"Gingerale, of course."

The Doctor sank into a chair and glanced idly at a calendar on the wall beside him. It showed the month of September. He lifted the calendar-sheet, but there was no page for October underneath it. "Strange. A village without a future . . ."

Morgan responded to this observation with the same blank stare that had greeted all the Doctor's earlier remarks. He was about to open another bottle of gingerale when the phone rang and he picked it up. "Fleur de Lys?" He listened for a moment and then looked at the Doctor. "I think it's for you, sir."

The Doctor took the receiver. "Hullo?"

"Doctor, is that you?"

"Well of course it is. Is that you, Sarah? What's happened? Where are you?"

Sarah's voice was hurried and urgent, and the words seemed to tumble out. "Listen, Doctor, Crayford caught me. They drugged me but I

55

woke up earlier than they expected, and I managed to escape. I heard them talking when they thought I was still out. I've found the whole plan. I can't come to the inn, it's one of their centers, so I came here."

"Sarah, where *are* you?"

"Village post office. You can cut through to it along the alleyway behind the pub. I'll wait for you here, but be careful. Those robot mechanics are everywhere."

"Don't worry, Sarah, I'll be careful. Who'd notice an inconspicuous chap like me anyway!" The Doctor put down the phone and turned to Morgan. "I've got to be going now. Thanks for your hospitality."

He turned to leave, then suddenly turned back, snatched up the phone and listened. "Well, would you believe it, it's out of order again!" With a farewell wave, the Doctor picked up the still unpoured gingerale bottle and shot out.

Styggron looked up as Chedaki marched impatiently into his control room, and demanded peevishly, "How much longer?"

Styggron went on checking instrument readings. "Once this experiment is concluded, we shall be ready."

Chedaki said impatiently, "Always one more experiment!"

"This is the last," said Styggron calmly. "The

Doctor is an ideal subject. It would be foolish to waste him."

"The longer he is allowed to live, the more he learns. The more he learns the more dangerous he becomes."

"You said I should not underestimate him, Chedaki, but I think you overestimate this Doctor. He is completely in my power."

"But he is unprogrammed, a free agent!"

"Only in appearance. In reality, he is trapped."

"I have studied his record with great care, Styggron. It is necessary to know the enemy. The Doctor has formidable intelligence, great resources, strange abilities . . ."

Styggron produced the dry croaking that is the Kraal form of laughter. "Stop, Chedaki, stop, or I shall be frozen with fear!"

"Oh, I know I am no scientist," said Chedaki angrily. "But a dead foe is a safe foe—every soldier knows that."

(The Kraals are a short-tempered race, and spend almost as much time fighting each other as in planning the conquest of other races. This ferocious temperament was the cause of the many savage atomic wars which had devastated their planet and reduced the Kraal race to a mere handful, totally dependent on the androids.)

Now Styggron too became angry. "Keep your imbecilic military maxims for your recruits, Marshal Chedaki. I shall destroy the Doctor in my own time—once he has served my purpose."

The closeness of zero hour made Chedaki nervous and tense, and he seemed perversely determined to find reasons to worry.

"If the androids fail in their task the Kraal invasion of Earth is doomed. Suppose the Doctor turns the androids against us? He could ruin the entire operation."

Styggron spoke with the weary patience of someone attempting to calm the irrational fears of a child. "That is impossible." He tapped the console. "The androids are all centrally governed. Their programming is controlled from here."

"Since the androids are programmed, they could be re-programmed. The Doctor has the knowledge. That is why he is so dangerous . . . The androids are a double-edged weapon, Styggron. They are unstoppable, indestructible."

Styggron stared impatiently at his frantic colleague. To some extent the Marshal was only expressing an old grievance. All Kraal soldiers resented the dominance of the scientists who ranked far above mere soldiers in Kraal society.

"The questions you raise have already been considered, Marshal Chedaki," said Styggron coldly. "Perhaps it is time for me to give you a demonstration."

They were interrupted by the entrance of Crayford. "Everything is ready, Styggron."

The Kraal scientist snapped, "Not quite, we need one more android. I am afraid we must call upon you for help in its production."

Crayford said wildly, "Please, Styggron, not again. I've been through it once. I can't stand the strain . . ."

"We need one more random unit, Crayford," said Styggron implacably. "We need an android programmed to attack Kraals. I am planning a little experiment to reassure the Marshal. Do not argue, Crayford. Come with me!"

Meekly Crayford followed the Kraals from the control room.

Crayford lay in a coffin-shaped plastic container, electrodes clamped to his temples. Not far away was another, similar container, at present empty. A complex web of electronic circuitry bridged the two. Styggron stood at a nearby control panel. Chedaki looked on impatiently.

Styggron's hand moved over the controls. "This should answer all your fears, Marshal Chedaki. From the suppressed hatred in Crayford's memory-cells we shall now create a totally hostile android." He touched a control.

Crayford screamed. "Don't, Styggron, I beg you . . ." His body arched and he lost consciousness as the power flooded through him.

A formless bubbling substance was flooding into the second container. It heaved and bubbled and hissed, half-gas, half-liquid. Styggron adjusted more controls. "I shall feed in the physical parameters of one of the Earth soldiers."

The substance in the other container solidified, took shape. Gradually it assumed the form of a soldier, dressed in combat gear, and armed with a rifle. The soldier's eyes snapped open and he stepped from the coffin.

"I shall now activate the hostility circuits," said Styggron calmly. The soldier sprang into a sudden crouch, his eyes sweeping round the room. At the sight of the two Kraals his eyes narrowed with hate. His gun swung up to cover them—and Styggron stepped forward. In his hand was an oddly shaped pistol with a bulbous handle. He fired and the weapon sprayed a fine mist around the attacking soldier. The soldier staggered back. He tried to raise the gun, but already his shape was beginning to blur. Styggron fired again and again, and the android soldier dissolved into a kind of globby puddle across the floor. Half-seen inside it was the spindly shape of the robot skeleton.

Styggron looked down in satisfaction. "You see, the androids are not immortal. What I can create, I can also destroy."

Chedaki was unable to keep the awe from his voice. "That weapon . . . It is new, Styggron?"

The Kraal scientist nodded. "Matter dispersion. So far it is effective only at short range. But we are developing a more powerful version for our space cruisers. Science, Marshal Chedaki! It is science that will make the Kraals invincible. Now if you have no further objections—may I continue my experiment with the Doctor?"

The Doctor reached the post office without incident, slipping along the lane that bordered the village. He walked round to the front of the building and went inside. The shop was the usual combination of newsstand, tobacconist and candyshop, with a counter across the back to mark off the post office. There were no lights on in the post office section, and the whole area was dark and shadowy.

A board creaked as the Doctor moved forwards, and suddenly a shape popped up from behind the counter. "Is that you, Doctor?"

"Of course it is, Sarah. What happened after I left you up that tree?"

Sarah leaned weakly against the counter. "I climbed down a bit too soon and those soldiers caught me. They knocked me out, and I woke up in a sort of operating theater. I was so frightened, Doctor."

"I'm sure you were," said the Doctor soothingly. "Here, have some gingerale!" He fished the bottle out of his pocket and handed it to her.

Sarah drank thirstily, and went on with her story. "Harry Sullivan was there, Doctor. Not the real Harry of course, but I thought it was."

"What do you mean—not the *real* Harry?"

"That's what they're doing, Doctor. They're copying people."

"Who are?"

"I don't really know. But Crayford was there too. I think he's behind it all somehow."

The Doctor shook his head. "No, it can't be Crayford. Not all by himself. Go on, what happened next?"

"There's not much more to tell. They put me in some kind of machine and I passed out."

"How did you get away?"

"When I came round for the second time I heard Crayford talking to someone. That's when I discovered what they're doing. They're replacing people with these duplicates they make. The must have thought I was still unconscious. They went off and left me without a guard and I managed to slip away."

The Doctor looked thoughtfully at her. "So you not only got away with suspicious ease, you were lucky enough to reach this place undetected *and* find the only telephone in the village that seems to work!"

Sarah backed away. "I don't understand."

"Don't you see, Sarah, they *let* you escape. They *let* you make that telephone call. We're being tested. They want to find out how smart we are."

Sarah rubbed a hand across her eyes. "No, Doctor, it can't be that."

"Of course it's that!" The Doctor rubbed his chin. "But if they're so technologically ad-

vanced they can make facsimile humans who'll
stand face-to-face examination, load them into
those canisters and send them through a space-
time warp to Earth—why should they be worried about us?"

Sarah stared blankly at him, as if she couldn't
take in what he was saying. The Doctor went
on, "They must possess the weaponry to attack
Earth by force. Instead they've created a
bridgehead by stealth using fake humans, these
androids." Suddenly he headed for the door.
"Coming, Sarah?"

"Where are we going?"

"To use the communications equipment in
the TARDIS." He hurried away.

Sarah called, "Coming, Doctor. Wait for me."
She hurried after him.

As if in confirmation of the Doctor's theory,
they made their way out of the village and
through the woods without seeing a soul. Once
a patrol of android mechanics passed by, heads
moving from side to side as if scanning the
countryside, but the Doctor and Sarah ducked
behind a tree trunk and the mechanics passed
them by.

Some time later, the Doctor stopped and
looked round. "We must be almost there by
now. The TARDIS should be just behind that
next clump of trees." But it wasn't. When they
reached the spot the TARDIS was nowhere to
be seen. "I'm sure it was here," said the Doctor.
"It was standing by that very tree."

Sarah looked round. "It's not here now, is it?" She shivered and buttoned up her jacket.

The Doctor seemed to be thinking aloud. "Well, it's not programmed to auto-operate. Unless of course . . ."

"Unless what?"

"When we landed here, I still had my doubts about where we were—so I set the TARDIS onto pause-control, with the coordinates for Earth locked into the guidance-system." He paused, then said abruptly, "Have you still got the TARDIS key, Sarah?"

Sarah shook her head. "I must have lost it."

The Doctor's voice hardened. "No! You haven't lost it because you never had it. Sarah came here and put the key in the lock, and left it there. That cancelled the pause control and the TARDIS continued on its set co-ordinates—back to Earth!"

Sarah looked at him as if he was mad. "I don't understand . . ."

"Oh yes you do," said the Doctor savagely. He pulled a twig from the nearest tree and snapped it in half. "This isn't wood, it's plastic. Those aren't real trees, this isn't real Earth—and you're not the real Sarah!"

64

7

The Countdown

As the Doctor moved forward, the android Sarah jumped back and pulled a gun from beneath her jacket. "Get back, Doctor."

"I began to suspect when I saw that jacket—a jacket I left under a bush! And you've buttoned it on the wrong side. You're a mirror-image Sarah—just like that mirror-image Harry, with his medals on the wrong side." The Doctor sprang forward, grasping the android's gun-arm and forcing it upwards. The gun exploded in the air, and the Doctor wrenched it from the android's hand, shaking his captive savagely. "Where's the real Sarah? What have you done with her? *Answer me!*"

The android broke free, tripped, and cannoned into the trunk of the nearest tree, hitting its head on the trunk. Horrifying, its "Sarah" face was jolted loose, rolling away across the ground. The Doctor looked down at the collapsed android. Packed into the skull cavity was a maze of wire and miniaturized transistors.

Sickened, he turned away—and the android's

65

fingers groped towards the gun butt which lay close to its hand. The Doctor heard the movement, spun round and a bullet whizzed close to his head. Ducking and weaving as he ran, the Doctor turned and fled.

The Doctor's retreating figure could be seen on the monitor screen in Styggron's control room. Chedaki said mockingly, "So much for your foolish experiment, Styggron. Now the Doctor is at large."

"There is no way of escape. He can do no harm." But there was a trace of uncertainty in Styggron's voice.

Chedaki seized his advantage. "Your experiment is at an end, Styggron. The androids are now fully trained, and the village simulation has served its purpose. It must be destroyed in precisely nine minutes and the Doctor with it."

Styggron seemed stunned by the Doctor's escape. "Nine minutes?"

"The invasion countdown has begun," Chedaki reminded him sternly. "There can be no variation in the schedule. You have arranged a safe method of destroying the training ground?"

"A matter-dissolving bomb. I shall place it in position myself."

"Excellent!" Chedaki turned to leave, and noticed a shrouded figure laying on a wheeled gurney. He bent to examine it. "This is the Earth female. Why is she still alive?"

66

"Another of my foolish experiments," said Styggron wearily. "The virus which our androids will use to cleanse Earth of its human population has been tested only in the laboratory. I wish to try it on a living organism. Now, shall we attend to the evacuation and destruction of the simulation?" He led the way out of the room, and Chedaki followed. As they left the sheet over the gurney was thrown back, and Sarah, the real Sarah, sat up. She had been conscious for some time, and had lain still, gathering her strength. She swung her legs down from the gurney and stood up. She was still a little shaky—but she could walk. "Nine minutes," she muttered. "Got to find the Doctor." Hurriedly she followed after the two Kraals.

The Doctor was moving cautiously through the deserted village when the wail of a siren shattered the peace of the empty street. A truck roared around the corner and parked in the center of the main street. People began emerging from the buildings, houses and shops and climbing into the back. Mr. Morgan appeared from the pub and got in with the others. As soon as the truck was full, it drove away.

The Doctor stepped out into the street and looked around. There was no one in sight. Now the village really was deserted.

* * *

Sarah followed the two Kraal leaders through a long gloomy tunnel. She heard the bustle of a crowd somewhere ahead of her. The tunnel led steeply upward to an open door, through which the entire population of the village seemed to be returning to the Kraals' underground headquarters. It was rather like Noah's ark. Crayford and Harry Sullivan stood and watched as villagers, soldiers and white-overalled mechanics marched in amd moved away. A last squad of soldiers came through, followed by Benton. "That's the lot, sir," he reported. "Everyone's inside."

Crayford nodded. "Good. See that all blast doors are closed, Sullivan. Styggron is placing the bomb now. It is due to explode in exactly four minutes."

"Yes, sir." Harry Sullivan, or rather his android replica, hurried away. Crayford touched a control and the door slid closed. Then he too moved off.

Sarah waited until everyone had gone, ran down the tunnel and went over to the door. She touched the control she'd seen Crayford use and the door slid open. She stepped outside and found herself in another long tunnel, sloping upwards. She followed it and emerged in an empty barn. The Kraals had hidden the entrance to their headquarters in a disused building.

Sarah was about to run off, when she paused, looking at the open door. She hunted around the door area and found a small control button set just above it. She pressed it and the door slid closed. Sarah turned and sprinted towards the village. She reckoned she had about three minutes to find the Doctor and bring him back to safety.

Blissfully unaware of his danger, the Doctor was wondering what to do next. He decided to go back to the Research Center and look for Sarah when the problem of his future was abruptly solved for him. He turned into a street that led towards the Research Center, and ran straight into Styggron. Immediately the Kraal's great paw flashed out and clamped round his arm. "I heard you coming, Doctor."

"With those ears, I'm not surprised." The Doctor tried to pull free but the grip on his arm was quite unbreakable.

"Resistance is inadvisable," growled Styggron. "We Kraals are the strongest species in the Galaxy."

"As well as the ugliest?" asked the Doctor impolitely. "Kraals, eh? So we're on Oseidon. And who might you be?"

"I am Styggron, Chief Scientist of the Kraals!" The Kraal began dragging the Doctor towards the village green. "Come. There is no time for pleasantries."

"How about unpleasantries, pig face?" said the Doctor rudely. He didn't much care for being hauled along like a reluctant toddler, but there was little he could do about it. Styggron dragged him to the war memorial that stood in the center of the village green. It took the form of a simple granite pillar on a low stone pedestal. Styggron slammed the Doctor against the piller with a force that knocked the breath from his body. Two white-coated mechanics appeared and lashed the Doctor to the pillar with a coil of plastic rope.

Styggron went away for a moment, and reappeared with a plain metal cylinder which he placed at the Doctor's feet. "I think you will find this unpleasant enough, Doctor."

The Doctor looked down. There was a simple timing dial set into the top of the cylinder, which gave off a steady 'beeping' sound. "A matter dispersal bomb?" asked the Doctor calmly.

"Exactly. In precisely three minutes everything within a radius of one-quarter Earth-mile will evaporate. Goodbye Doctor!"

Styggron turned away.

"You're not leaving already," called the Doctor plaintively. Styggron ignored him, and disappeared between the buildings. The mechanics followed.

The Doctor began struggling furiously, but the plastic had some kind of self-binding quality. The more he struggled the tighter it became.

At his feet the bomb beeped steadily away.

70

To his astonishment he heard a voice some-where in the distance. "Doctor, can you hear me? Where are you?"

"Sarah, over here!" yelled the Doctor, and a few seconds later Sarah came running across the green towards him. She was shouting as she ran, "Doctor, they're going to blow this place sky-high any minute. Don't just stand there—come on!"

"I am not just standing here," said the Doctor with dignity. "If you'll look a little closer . . ."

Sarah saw the plastic ropes fastening the Doctor to the war memorial, the ticking bomb at his feet. "Oh no," she gasped and began wrestling with his bonds.

But the plastic had a life of its own and it seemed to fight against her fingers. "Find the free end and give one steady pull," said the Doctor calmly.

Sarah did her best, but the plastic seemed de-termined not to budge. "How long have we got?"

"A little over a minute. I think you'd better give up and save yourself, Sarah."

"No, I've got it . . . it's coming." The plastic coil began to pull away at last, and Sarah un-wound with panic-stricken haste. As the Doctor stepped down Sarah grabbed his hand. "Come on, Doctor, run. There's only one place we'll be safe."

The bomb timer was already measuring off its last few seconds.

* * *

Styggron glared angrily at the empty gurney. He returned to his console and touched a communicator switch. "The Earth girl has escaped. Find her." He paused and checked his instruments. "The countdown to matter-dispersion has entered final phase." He began counting off the last few seconds. "Zero minus sixty . . . fifty-nine . . . fifty-eight . . ." Magnified by the communication system, Styggron's voice boomed through the Kraal base. On his monitor screen the village of Devesham basked peacefully in the sun.

The Doctor and Sarah sprinted across a field and into the barn. Sarah hurried to the corner and opened the hatch that concealeed the Kraal tunnel.

As they ran down the steep tunnel they could hear a voice chanting. "Ten . . . nine . . . eight . . . seven . . ."

They reached the blast-door at the end of the tunnel at last and Sarah groped in the darkness for the control. "Six . . . five . . . four . . ." chanted the voice.

The door slid back and the Doctor and Sarah dived through. The magnified voice boomed in their ears. "Three . . . two . . . one . . ." A shattering explosion rocked the corridor, knocking them both off their feet . . .

(In Styggron's control room, the peaceful village scene faded from the monitor. It was replaced by a barren rocky landscape—the natural surface of Oseidon).

Dislodged rock was still falling from the ceiling as the Doctor and Sarah picked themselves up. "A close-run thing," said the Doctor solemnly.

"I wouldn't care to have run it any closer——" Sarah broke off as Crayford and a squad of soldiers appeared at the end of the corridor. The Doctor and Sarah turned to run, but Harry Sullivan and more soldiers were blocking the way behind them.

The Doctor looked at Sarah, and they raised their hands. They were prisoners again, but at least they were alive. "Take them to the detention cell," ordered Crayford. "I must report to Styggron."

"That's the warty chap with the big nose, isn't it?" said the Doctor conversationally.

"Move," snapped the android, and the soldiers bustled them off.

As they were being led away, the Doctor said, "I perfer our version of Harry, don't you, Sarah? Much better mannered."

On Styggron's monitor, the barren landscape of Oseidon was replaced by a rocketship.

Marshal Chedaki's voice came over the communicator. "Leader rocket ship in launch frame."

"Have the pre-launch checks been completed?"

"Yes, Styggron. The androids are being loaded now."

Crayford hurried in. "Styggron, we have recaptured the girl." He paused. "The Doctor was with her."

Styggron swung round, the deep-set eyes flaring with anger. "The Doctor? I destroyed him with the village."

"It seems he escaped."

Styggron turned back to his controls. "He must be disposed of. Kill him, immediately. Kill them both!"

8

Braindrain

Crayford stared at the Kraal leader in distress. "Kill them? Surely that's no longer necessary."

"You sing a different song now, Crayford," jeered Styggron. "They must be eliminated. Isn't that what you said?"

Crayford was aware that somehow his feelings had changed. "When I thought they were a danger to the plan, yes. But the preliminary stage is over now. What harm can they do locked in a detention cell?"

Styggron said indifferently, "The Doctor is no longer of any use to me."

"You're wrong, Styggron. He would make a valuable subject for your braindrain machine."

"To what purpose?"

"He's a brilliant man—a genius. All his knowledge and experience would make a useful addition to your data banks."

Styggron said scornfully, "You were prepared to accept his death provided that I killed him. You are squeamish, Crayford, a puny weakling, like all your race."

"Think what you like, Styggron. But you gave me your word. You said no one would be harmed unnecessarily."

Styggron turned away. "Oh very well, very well. Let him live for now."

"Thank you, Styggron."

As Crayford left the control room Styggron muttered, "I shall drain every atom of knowledge from his brain—and *then* he shall die!"

The Doctor was busily attacking the cell door with his sonic screwdriver, though without much success. As he worked he did his best to explain the Kraal plan to Sarah, who was finding it difficult to take in.

"*Not* Earth, Doctor? What do you mean?"

"Surely you've realized by now? Harry and Benton and all the others aren't real people at all."

"Not real?"

"Fakes," said the Doctor patiently. "Copies. Electronic and mechanical androids, with programmed computers instead of brains. If I'd had my wits about me I'd have realized earlier. Remember that high radiation level I noticed when we first left the TARDIS? Oseidon, the planet of the Kraals, is the only inhabited planet in the galaxy with a level that high. The Kraals fought one atomic war too many. Not many of them survived it—and they ruined their planet into the bargain." He turned from the door in disgust. "No good, I can't shift it."

"There's an armed sentry outside anyway——" Sarah interrupted herself. "Radiation? Won't we get radiation sickness or something?"

"I doubt it, we weren't exposed for long enough."

Sarah shuddered. "Still, the sooner we get away from here the better."

"That's what the Kraals think. You see the radiation level on this planet isn't just high, it's unstable, increasing all the time. It won't be too long before the place is uninhabitable, even for the few Kraals that are left. That's why they're planning to leave and take over the Earth."

"So everything we've seen here has been a fake?"

"That's right. The woods, the Research Center, even the village. Everything copied down to the last detail—including the inhabitants!"

"But why? As a sort of training ground?"

"Exactly. They've made hardly a slip. Oh, one or two minor details were wrong, like mint-fresh coins all with the same date. But otherwise they got nearly everything right."

The door was flung open and Crayford came into the cell. They caught a glimpse of Corporal Adams on guard outside, then the door closed. Crayford said abruptly, "I've been listening to you—I was just outside."

"Bad habit, eavesdropping," said the Doctor reprovingly. "Still, no one's perfect."

77

Crayford stared wildly at them. He felt a strange need to talk to the two prisoners, to explain things, to justify himself—but somehow he didn't know where to begin. Still in the same jerky fashion he said, "So, you're impressed with the thoroughness of this operation?"

"It's impressive right enough," agreed the Doctor. "Doomed to fail though, all the same."

For some reason Crayford felt it was important to convince the Doctor that he was wrong. "No, Doctor. Very shortly I shall be leaving for Earth. The Kraals will project me through their space-time warp, and my ship will make a normal re-entry through Earth's atmosphere."

"A normal re-entry?" said the Doctor skeptically. "You've been away for two years. They gave you up for dead."

Crayford gave a triumphant smile. "That's where you're wrong, Doctor. Not long ago I re-established radio contact with Earth. I told them about the stablizer failure that sent my ship out beyond Jupiter. I told them how I'd rationed my provisions, rigged up re-cycling apparatus. Every telescope on Earth is trained on the sky waiting for the gallant XK5 to reappear."

"A hoax," said the Doctor softly. "A giant hoax."

"Exactly. All planned by Styggron, Chief Scientist of the Kraals."

"Helped by you. He couldn't have done any

of it without drawing on your memories, your knowledge."

Crayford said, "The superb technology of the Kraals——"

Sarah interrupted him. "Why did you do it? What made you betray Earth to the Kraals?"

"And didn't Earth betray *me*?" shouted Crayford hysterically. "I was sent out with faulty equipment and then written off, abandoned, left to die in space. It was the Kraals who saved me. I was dying, torn apart by gyro-failure. They re-created me, Miss Smith. Re-created me in every detail—except for this one eye which couldn't be found." Crayford rubbed nervously at the black eye-patch. "I owe the Kraals everything."

"And that's what they want in return," said Sarah bitterly. "Everything. They want the world—and you're giving it to them."

"The Kraals are a doomed race. They must leave their own planet because of the radiation level. Why should a race with such skills be left to die?"

"Earth has one or two skills of its own," said the Doctor gently.

"The Kraals have promised me no humans will be harmed—as long as they accept the ultimatum. The Kraals will take the northern hemisphere of the planet and live in peace. I have their word."

The Doctor looked sadly at him. "And you really believe that? You've been brainwashed,

79

Crayford. Although I think it's starting to wear off a little . . ."

Stubbornly Crayford shook his head. "Before my ship lands the space shells containing the androids will be launched. If they are seen, they'll be taken for meterorites. The androids will take over the Space Research Center and Marshal Chedaki will be able to bring in the invasion fleet without detection. Not a shot will be fired."

"If your Kraal friends are so peace-loving, why did Styggron try to blow me up with the village?"

"He thought you were a danger to the plan. Miss Smith's memory-print revealed your past involvement with the defense of Earth." Crayford paused, rubbing nervously at his eyepatch. "Styggron still thinks you're dangerous. I've managed to persuade him to utilize your knowledge rather than waste it. He has a machine that extracts the entire memory and intelligence of any living creature, and feeds it into a computer. It's a painful process, Doctor— but it's better than dying."

A Kraal voice crackled over the communication-system. "Service mechanics to leader rocket loading bay."

Crayford went and rapped on the door. "It's time for me to go. Believe me, Doctor, I know what I'm doing." The door opened and Crayford went out.

The Doctor stared hard at the locked cell

door. "I've got to get to Earth and warn them."

"How?" asked Sarah despairingly. "We haven't even got the TARDIS any more."

The Doctor was staring into space. In his mind a plan was forming. It was insanely risky—but it might be the only chance to save Earth.

Marshal Chedaki came bustling into Styggron's laboratory. "The launch count-down is about to begin——" He broke off in surprise. A metal tray stood incongruously on top of the control console. It contained a jug apparently full of water, a cup, and a platter on which rested some chunks of coarse bread. Standing over the tray were Styggron, and the Harry Sullivan android. It was taking the stopper from a plastic phial. "Carefully," hissed Styggron. "Only one drop. Handle it *carefully*." It was clear that the Kraal scientist was in a state of tense excitement.

Suddenly Chedaki understood. "This is the culture you spoke of?"

"Yes, Marshal. This little phial holds the death-sentence of the human race."

The android allowed one drop of colourless liquid to drip from the phial into the water-jug. "Be careful," said Styggron again.

His evident nervousness affected Chedaki. "Is the virus safe to handle?"

"As long as only the androids come into contact with it. You do well to be concerned, Chedaki. Even we Kraals are not immune to its effect."

With some relief Chedaki watched the android reseal the phial and place it in a sterilizing chamber. "Now, take the tray to the detention cell," ordered Styggron. "We shall test it on the girl."

The Doctor had abandoned his attempts to open the door, and was attacking the floor instead. He had succeeded in lifting one of the metal plates, and was at work on the tangle of electric cables underneath. "This has possibilities, Sarah, distinct possibilities."

"What are you trying to do?"

"Androids work through electronic circuitry. If we can lure that guard in here and give him a good stiff jolt . . ." The Doctor heaved a length of cable from the tangle of wires, breaking one end free.

"Electrocute him?"

"Well, randomize him, to be strictly accurate. He's only a machine, remember."

Sarah heard footsteps along the corridor. "Someone coming, Doctor."

The Doctor thrust the loose cable back into the gap and slid the cover plate into position, hoping no one would notice it wasn't fastened. The door opened and the Harry Sullivan android came into the cell carrying a tray. "Styggron sends you this." He put the tray down on the bunk.

The Doctor looked at it. "How very thoughtful. Bread and water, I see. Traditional prisoners' fare."

"It's better than nothing," said Sarah. "And I'm thirsty." She poured water into the cup.

The android turned to the Doctor. "You will come with me." It took the Doctor's wrist in a painful grip.

The Doctor winced. "Careful! You androids don't know your own strength!"

"Come," said the android tonelessly. It began dragging the Doctor away.

Sarah was just about to drink the water, but at this new development she put down the cup. "Where are you taking him?"

The android didn't answer, but the Doctor shouted, "Treat that water with caution, Sarah—and don't waste it. Water's an excellent conductor, remember!"

The door slammed behind him. Sarah looked at the loose plate on the floor, and then at the tray. She reached for the water jug.

The Doctor looked curiously around Styggron's laboratory. "So this is where you put Crayford back together again! Careless of you to lose his eye, wasn't it?"

Styggron gestured towards the operating table. "Hurry. I have little time."

83

The android dragged the Doctor towards the table. The Doctor made a desperate attempt to break free, but the android forced him onto the table with unconcerned ease.

"Leaving soon, are you, Styggron?" gasped the Doctor.

"Very soon, Doctor." Styggron moved over to the table and began securing clamps to hold the Doctor in place. The Doctor struggled wildly, but against the combined strengths of Kraal and android he was completely helpless.

Sarah finished sloshing the water in the jug around the door. She picked up the cup, hesitated for a moment. One cupful wouldn't make much difference. She remembered the Doctor's warning and poured the cup of water onto the floor.

Lifting up the floor-plate, she pulled out the cable. One end was free, and presumably, live. Now all she needed was some way to get the guard in the cell. She could yell, of course, but he'd probably ignore her . . . She thought hard for a moment then slipped the brightly colored scarf from around her neck.

Cautiously she rubbed the ends of the cable against the metal floor-strut. There was a shower of sparks. She did it again, holding the scarf near the end of the cable. The scarf charred and began to smoke. Eagerly Sarah blew on it, fanning the glowing red sparks into flame.

Despite his struggles, the Doctor was now firmly secured to the operating table, held down with clamps so that he could scarcely wriggle. The Sullivan android had gone, and Styggron was fastening electrodes to the Doctor's head.

"In a moment, Doctor, the knowledge and experience of your entire life will be transposed into our data bank."

"That's stealing," said the Doctor indignantly.

"And while you are making your small contribution to Kraal culture, I shall be on my way to destroy the humans you have so often defended." Styggron looked mockingly down at the Doctor. "This time you will be powerless to help them."

"So, you intend genocide, do you?"

"Earth's resources are limited," said Styggron indifferently. "They cannot be wasted in the support of an inferior species."

"And just how do you plan to wipe out the human race? Nuclear fission will raise Earth's radiation level above even your tolerance."

"Nothing so crude, Doctor. The androids will spread a virus that will rid Earth of its human population within weeks. The virus is self-limiting. It will burn itself out, and Earth will be ours."

"And where will you be while all this is going on?"

"Crayford's rocket will automatically be placed in quarantine. I shall remain inside until it is time to signal Marhsal Chedaki to bring in the invasion fleet."

"The best-laid schemes of mice and Kraals gang aft agley," said the Doctor defiantly. "Something will go wrong, Styggron!"

"Nothing can go wrong." Styggron pulled a switch and the Doctor's ears were filled by a high-pitched electronic buzz that seemed to echo around his brain. Multi-colored lights began flashing in front of his eyes and the laboratory seemed to be spinning around him.

Styggron made a final adjustment to his instruments. "In a few minutes, Doctor, the analyzer will have completed its recording. To avoid harming the subject, it must then be switched off. Unfortunately, I shall not be here. Your brain-tissue will expand under the stimulation until your head explodes. I imagine it is a most unpleasant death."

The Doctor's face was twisted with strain, as he marshalled all his strength to resist the effects of the machine. Styggron laughed. "Defiant to the last, I see, Doctor. Soon you will be screaming for mercy. And there will be no one here!"

9

Blast Off

Sarah held the smoldering scarf close to the grille in the cell door and blew frantically. Would the guard even notice the smoke drifting out into the corridor? If he did, would he feel it his duty to investigate? A human guard might, but who could tell how an android would react?

Suddenly she heard the sound of bolts being drawn back. Dropping the scarf she stepped back and picked up the cable.

The door swung open and Corporal Adams came through the doorway, his booted feet in the puddle of water around the door. He raised his rifle—and Sarah jabbed the end of the cable against the metal barrel of the gun.

The results were spectacular. The android went rigid. It staggered back, arms and legs flailing wildly, puffs of smoke coming from its body as connections overloaded and blew up. It gave a final convulsive jerk, then dropped to the ground like a puppet with severed strings.

Sarah looked down in horror. The android's

entire chest had exploded and she could see a smoking tangle of wires and circuits inside its torso. Leaping over the android, and over the puddle of water in which it lay, Sarah set off to look for the Doctor.

Styggron looked with satisfaction at the writhing form on the table. The Doctor was resisting the effects of the braindrain machine for an amazingly long time, but soon he would have to give way. Styggron wished he could stay and watch the process, but on the eve of the invasion he had many other duties. Reluctantly he left the laboratory.

Sarah turned a corner just in time to see Styggron come out of the laboratory and move away. She dodged back, waited until he was out of sight, then ran into the laboratory.

To her horror, she saw the Doctor stretched out on the operating table, body writhing and face twisted with strain. She ran to the console and began turning off every control in sight. In a few seconds the electronic howling died away, and the the Doctor slumped back unconscious.

Sarah began unfastening the clamps that held him to the table. When she'd finished, the Doctor was still unconscious. In desperation she slapped his face to revive him. He opened his eyes and looked reproachfully at her. "Ouch— that hurt!"

"Come on, Doctor. You've got to wake up."

"I `am awake, I think," said the Doctor dreamily. "Once upon a time there were three sisters and they lived at the bottom of a well. Their names were Olga, Marsha and Irene. Are you listening, Tilly?"

Sarah shook him by the shoulder. "Wake up, Doctor, this is no time for fairy-stories. And I'm Sarah! You're in the Kraals' laboratory."

The dreamy look faded from the Doctor's face and he swung his legs down from the table. "Yes, that seems to make sense. Come on, Sarah, we've got to hurry!"

"Where to?"

"Crayford's rocket. It'll be leaving for Earth any minute—and we're going with it!"

As they ran along the corridors they heard the dull roaring of the rocket motors. The Doctor ran steadily towards the sound, using it as a guide. They came to a long corridor with a heavy door at the end, ran through it, and found themselves in the open air.

They were in a huge square launching bay, a kind of concrete pit. In the center of it, supported by a metal gantry, was the XK5, the rocket ship in which Crayford had been sent off to explore the universe.

A magnified Kraal voice was ringing through the area. "Launching area should now be cleared. Time to lift off, zero minus sixty . . ."

The rocket's motors were running up to launch point, and a blast of exhaust gases swirled through the launch area like a desert wind. Sarah backed away, but the Doctor yelled, "Come on!" He grabbed her by the wrist and began dragging her towards the rocket.

When they reached it, the Doctor began swarming up the metal gantry that supported the rocket. Frightened as she was, Sarah had to follow. It was a long and terrifying climb. Finally the Doctor edged along a narrow metal beam, and wrestled with a hatch until he got it open. "This should take us into the cargo hold. In you go, Sarah." He helped Sarah through, scrambled in after her, and closed the hatch.

They were in a metal chamber about the size of a small room. Its walls were lined with racks upon which rested long coffin-like shapes. The racks had metal caterpillar tracks on them, and the whole effect was rather like that of a bomb-bay.

The Doctor hurried towards the canisters and wrenched open first one and then another. Androids lay corpse-like inside the shells, a motherly looking women and a middle-aged man. Sarah jumped back and the Doctor grinned. "It's all right, these ones aren't activated yet." He grabbed the man android and chucked it casually aside. "Quick, Sarah, in you get!"

"What for?"

"Protection. The G-force will be crushing

when the ship blasts off. We'll have to use these as acceleration-couches."

The Doctor helped Sarah into the shell, dumped the second android and climbed in himself. Lying back in the chair, he waited calmly for take-off.

A Kraal voice boomed through the ship. "Time to lift off, fifteen seconds. Close vents!" They braced themselves. The voice came again. "Ten . . . nine . . . eight . . . seven . . . six . . . five . . . four . . . three . . . two . . . one . . ."

The roar of the rocket motors rose to a shrieking crescendo. Sarah felt a giant invisible hand crushing her down into the shell. It pressed harder, harder, until her whole body seemed flattened by the enormous strain. "It's crushing me . . ." she gasped, and everything went black . . .

She awoke to find the Doctor looking down at her. "Time to wake up, Sarah, we're on our way."

Slowly and painfully, Sarah sat up. Every inch of her body seemed to be bruised. "I must have blocked out."

"The G-force cut the blood supply to what you humans laughingly refer to as your higher centers."

Sarah groaned and climbed out of the shell. "I hate sarcasm, especially when I'm dying. I feel as if I've been put through a mangle."

"Never mind," said the Doctor cheerfully.

"That was a gentle massage compared to what's ahead."

"Don't tell me," implored Sarah. "I don't want to know."

"Of course you do," said the Doctor cheerfully. "Now listen carefully. Just before Crayford brings his ship into re-entry orbit, these containers will be shot out through those cargo-shuttle ejectors like seeds from a lemon—and we'll be in them."

"Oh will we? Why?"

"Because the space-shells will reach Earth before the ship—and there's no other way we can get a warning to the Space Research Center—the real one, I mean."

"And what do we use for air?"

The Doctor was examining a couple of tiny rocket-vents set into the side of one of the shells. "There'll be enough air in the containers to last the few minutes in space. I'm more concerned about the efficiency of the retro-tubes."

"You mean they might not work?" asked Sarah nervously. The more she heard about this scheme, the more risky it sounded.

"Oh, I imagine they'll work all right—enough for androids to survive impact. Kraal technology is pretty reliable on the whole. But we may be in for a nasty jolt as we come down."

"I see," said Sarah, summing up. "So, providing we don't burn up on re-entry, and aren't suffocated on the way down, we'll probably be smashed to bits when we land?"

The Doctor said solemnly, "You've put your finger on the one tiny flaw in our plan."

"*Our* plan? This is *your* plan, Doctor!"

"Well, if you've got any better ideas, I'm open to suggestions."

Sarah thought hard for a moment, then shook her head. "How long before all this starts?"

The Doctor's face was grave. "Quite soon, I'm afraid, Sarah. The Kraals must be beaming us through the space-time warp now. We'll soon be close to Earth."

In the scanner room of the Space Research Center (the *real* Space Research Center, not the now-exploded Kraal reconstruction) there was an air of scarcely-suppressed excitement. Technicians sat hunched over their instrument panels, each wanting to be the one to spot the returning spaceman. One of them, a girl called Tessa, was peering excitedly at a shadowy, hardly-visible spot on her scanner-screen. Was it a genuine sighting, or just a ghost-signal? At last she could keep silent no longer. "I think I've got him, sir. Bearing one four three."

Almost immediately another technician said, "Contact confirmed, bearing one four three." There was a babble of relief and excitement.

Grierson, the burly chief technician, said, "Well done, Tessa." He leaned forward to his communicator-mike. "Colonel Faraday? This is the scanner room. We've picked up Crayford's ship. Yes, sir, absolutely on schedule."

Harry Sullivan and Benton (the *real* Harry Sullivan and Benton) walked along the corridor of the Space Research Center deep in conversation. They'd followed Brigadier Lethbridge-Stewart there on his temporary assignment as head of station security, and had been left behind when some crisis in the affairs of UNIT whipped the Brigadier off to Geneva. Now they were with Colonel Faraday, his replacement, a likeable enough old chap, but, in Harry's view, a bit of a fusspot.

"I don't like it, sir," Benton was saying. "The TARDIS turns up in the woods by itself, but no Doctor! And where's Miss Smith?" Benton was fond of Sarah, and took a protective interest in her.

Harry shrugged. He hadn't known the Doctor as long as Benton—but long enough to feel that nothing the Doctor did could surprise him any more.

Worriedly Benton went on, "We've searched the area for them and made enquiries in the village. Not a sign of 'em. Suppose they're in some kind of trouble?"

"You're a pessimist, Mr. Benton," said Harry cheerfully. "The Doctor can look after himself. Besides, what could possibly happen to him in Devesham Wood?"

Benton shook his head. "I don't know. It's just I've never known him to leave the TARDIS with the key in it before."

As they were passing one of the side-entrances a portly self-important figure in army uniform shot through the doorway and bumped into them. "Ah, there you are, you two. Crayford's just been picked up on the scanners. Come along, men." Faraday hurried away, and the other two followed.

Benton was still worrying. He was glad they'd got their lost astronaut back all right. But what had happened to the Doctor and Sarah?

They followed Faraday into the scanner room and Grierson hurried forward. "There's Crayford's ship, sir, on the master scanner."

Faraday studied the little blip on the giant screen. "Fantastic. This is a moment that will go down in history, Grierson."

"That it is, sir."

"A two-year journey, eh? He's been farther out into space than any other human being."

"We're trying to raise him on audio now, sir."

A technician was leaning over the long-range communicator. "Hullo XK5, Hullo XK5, this is Devesham Control calling XK5, do you read?"

There was a moment's tense silence, then a voice crackled weakly from the loud speaker. "Hello, Devesham Control, this is XK5, I'm receiving you."

Grierson indicated the speaker-mike to Faraday. "Sir, would you care to say something?"

Faraday leaned forward and sputtered, "Hullo, Crayford! This is Colonel Faraday. What can I possibly say at a time like this except . . . welcome home!"

"Thank you, sir, Earth certainly looks good. I've had some problems with . . ." There was a crackle of static and the voice faded away.

Before Faraday could answer Tessa called excitedly, "Look, sir, on the scanner!"

A tiny cluster of dots was rushing through space. Faraday turned to Grierson. "Is that him? Has he started re-entry?"

It was Tessa who answered. "Not yet, sir. Something else is coming in the same flight-path."

"Something else?" demanded Faraday irritably. "What? What is it, Tessa?"

"Difficult to say, sir. Could be a fireball, or a shower of meteorites. Whatever they are, they're heading straight for Earth."

10

Hero's Return

The XK5 was on its way down to Earth now—
and the modifications built in by the Kraal
technicians were coming into effect. In the
leading bay the space shells slid one by one
across the racks and towards the launching
tubes. Two more jolted towards the exit point.
Sarah lay in one, the Doctor in the other.

Sarah clenched her teeth in an effort not to
scream as she felt her canister slide towards the
launch tube. There was a rumble, a jolt, and she
felt herself dropping into endless space . . .

The Doctor lay in his canister, stretched out
calm and relaxed. At least it was a novel way to
travel, he thought. The space-shell trundled
along the tracks into the tube. Seconds later the
Doctor too was hurtling down towards Earth.

In the scanner room the freak meteor shower
was still baffling Grierson. "They're down to
seventeen thousand now, sir."

"Never mind the wretched meteorites," bellowed Faraday. "Have you still got a fix on the ship?"

"She's just hit the upper atmosphere, sir," said Grierson soothingly. "Looks as if she's on a perfect re-entry path. Don't worry, sir, he'll be back in the mess in time for breakfast."

"Oh no he won't," growled Faraday. "Not after two years in unknown space. That's why I'm here. He'll go straight into quarantine, him and his ship."

Benton edged closer to Tessa, who was still studying the meteor swarm. "Don't they usually burn up before they hit Earth?"

She nodded. "This lot aren't going to though. There's something funny about them."

"What do you mean—funny?"

"Well, I'd swear they're slowing down—and that's impossible!"

Like a flock of strange birds the space-shells hissed down over Devesham woods. Most dropped in or near the quarry, others overshot and crashed down amongst the trees.

Before long a number of shells lay scattered at the edge of the quarry. One of them rocked and sprang open, and the Doctor clambered stiffly out, looking around him. There was no telling which of the other space shells held Sarah, and if he started opening them at random he might have to cope with the attack of

98

some re-activated android. Sarah would have to make her own way to safety.

The Doctor turned and hurried through the woods. All round him was the whistle and thump of the descending space shells.

Inside the control room, the atmosphere of excitement returned. Things were entering the last, most dangerous phase now, the landing itself. The ship was to be brought down to a "hard" landing on the little rocket-field that adjoined the Space Research Center. A single mistake and the returning astronaut would be dashed to pieces against the planet he had waited so long to reach. Everyone's eyes were fixed on the master scanner. Re-entry into the Earth's atmosphere was the trickiest time. A failure in the heat shielding and the ship could flare into nothingness like a meteor. Suddenly, Crierson snapped, "That's it, sir. He's made it. He's through!"

A voice came through the speaker. "XK5 to Control. This is XK5 calling Control."

Grierson leaned over the mike. "Devesham Control to XK5. We're locking on."

"Roger, Devesham, I copy."

Grierson's voice was calm and level. He might have been carrying out the simplest of test routines. "Ignition minus thirty seconds. On my mark, mark."

Crayford's voice came back equally relaxed.

"Mark thirty, Devesham. AGS reading, four hundred plus one."

"Ten seconds to ignition."

There was a long, tense pause. Then, "I have ignition, Devesham. Commencing descent."

A technician's voice began droning out the instrument readings. "Altitude forty thousand meters . . . thirty nine . . . thirty eight thousand . . . Descent velocity six-fifty meters per second . . ."

Faraday turned to Harry Sullivan. "He'll be landing in just a few seconds, Sullivan, I'll want you to give him the preliminary check-up. Got everything you need?"

Harry held up the traditional black bag. "The tools of the trade are all in here, sir."

"Good man . . ."

Grierson said, "You're looking good, Commander Crayford."

"Things look good to me too. Got the champagne on ice, have you?"

"Ready and waiting." Grierson's voice became formal again. "You are cleared for landing, XK5."

"Roger, Devesham. Beginning final descent now."

The technician began reading off more figures. "Coming down at five hundred meters . . . four hundred . . . two-fifty . . . two hundred. Slight drift to the right . . ."

"Correcting now," snapped Grierson.

Then Crayford's voice. "Descent completed.

Engine command override off. Engine arm off . . . That's it, gentlemen. Open up the bubbly."

An excited babble of congratulations filled the control room. Grierson's voice cut through the chatter as he turned to Faraday. "The XK5 has landed, sir." He smiled for the first time. "Now it's over to you—and I can't say I'm sorry!"

Faraday slapped him on the back. "Well done, my dear fellow. Well done! Come on, Sullivan, we'll go on board straight away."

Faraday bustled Harry out of the room, and Grierson said, "Commander Crayford? Colonel Faraday and the Medical Officer are on their way up to you now."

On the flight deck of his rocket, Crayford was stretching in his chair. "Thanks Control, I'll be waiting. Don't forget that champagne!"

He glanced up at Styggron, who stood waiting behind his chair. The Kraal scientist smiled. "Good Crayford. As you say, we shall be waiting."

The Doctor hurried up to the main entrance to the Space Research Center, hoping that none of the androids had arrived before him. The precise arrival point of the shells was a matter of pure chance, and if some had landed very close to the Center . . . This time everything was as it should be. There were armed sentries at the gate, and Corporal Adams came hurrying out to meet him. "Can you tell me where I can find Colonel Faraday?" demanded the Doctor.

"I think he's in the scanner room, sir." The Doctor made to go inside, and Corporal Adams said firmly, "Excuse me, sir, I'll need to see your pass."

The Doctor fished through a number of pockets and finally managed to produce the special pass the Brigadier had given him. It was lucky he still had the thing. He hated identification papers and passes, and usually managed to lose them.

Adams checked the pass carefully. "Very good, sir. You can go ahead."

"Thank you." The Doctor set off for the main steps and then turned back. "Do you know who I am?"

"Yes, sir, Scientific Adviser, aren't you? You came here once with Brigadier Lethbridge-Stewart."

"That's right. Now, listen carefully. Is this the first time you've seen me today?"

"What's that, sir?"

"It's a simple enough question, surely. Is this the first time I've been in here today?"

"Yes sir," said Adams woodenly.

The Doctor nodded, satisfied. "Good, now if you should see me again today, I want you to report it to me immediately. I'll be with Colonel

Faraday." The Doctor disappeared inside the building.

Adams stared after him. Talk about your mad scientists . . .

In the scanner room everything was winding down. Technicians were sipping machine-made coffee and discussing the recent landing. In the corner, Benton was busy with a personal telephone call. "Okay, then," he was saying, "eight o'clock outside the Chinese takeout. And don't be late."

"You've got her well-trained," said Grierson cheerfully.

Benton looked embarrassed. "It's my kid sister. She's coming down to see me this evening. I promised to take her to the village dance." He broke off in astonishment as the Doctor sailed into the room. "Doctor, where on earth have you been?"

The Doctor grinned and shook him by the hand. "Not on Earth at all, actually."

"You realize we've had search-parties out for you——" began Benton indignantly.

The Doctor interrupted him. "Where's Colonel Faraday?"

"Gone over to the rocket with Mr. Sullivan. You know Commander Crayford's just landed, Doctor?"

"I do indeed," said the Doctor grimly. "Now listen, we've got to stop them." He turned to

Grierson who had been looking on in amazement. "Call them back."

Grierson was shocked. "I can't do that, Doctor. The Colonel would be furious . . ."

The Doctor looked ready to explode and Benton said warningly, "Better do as the Doctor says, sir. He usually knows what he's doing. I'll take the responsibility."

"Very well, if you're sure." Grierson went to the microphone. "Hullo, Devesham Control to rocket field. Is Colonel Faraday there?"

A voice said, "He's in the rocket elevator with Doctor Sullivan."

Grierson adjusted a monitor screen, and tapped the Doctor's arm. "I'm afraid you're too late, Doctor. Look!"

On the screen they could see Crayford's XK5 rocket standing in the middle of the little field. A support gantry had been wheeled in place around it, and they could see the tiny cabin of the elevator by the rocket entrance.

The Doctor pushed Grierson aside. "You at the rocket field! Is there a communication set up in that elevator?"

"Why, yes sir, but . . ."

"Then patch me through to them—now!"

Such was the authority in the Doctor's voice that the man obeyed without question. There was a crackle and a voice said, "You're through to the elevator now, sir."

"Hullo! Harry Sullivan!" said the Doctor urgently. "Harry, can you hear me?"

104

Harry's astonished voice said, "Doctor! Is that you?"

"Yes it is! *Don't get into that rocket!*"

They heard another voice in the background. "I don't understand? What's going on, Sullivan?"

"Just trust me, Colonel Faraday," shouted the Doctor. "If you go into that rocket you'll be in the most terrible danger—and so will the rest of the planet!"

11

Takeover

For a moment nothing came from the other end but an astonished silence. Then they heard the rumble of Colonel Faraday's voice. "I don't understand, Sullivan. What's the matter with this chap? He must be insane!"

There was a soothing mumble from Harry Sullivan, more spluttered expostulations from Faraday. Then they heard Harry say, "Really sir, I think we'd better do as the Doctor says. We can always come back after we've found out what's worrying him. After all, Commander Crayford's already waited two years. He won't be worried about a minute or two longer!"

To the Doctor's relief he heard Faraday mumble, "Oh very well then."

"Bring that elevator down now, Harry," said the Doctor. "I'll explain the whole thing when you get back here."

He heard Faraday's voice "Very well, Doctor, we'll do as you say. But your explanation had better be a good one."

Grierson pointed to the monitor. "Look, the elevator's started down again, Doctor."

The Doctor gave a sigh of relief. Perhaps he'd arrived in time after all.

A technician popped his head into the scanner room. "Mr. Benton, there's a call for you. Could you take it on the corridor phone?"

Benton groaned. Probably his sister, saying she'd missed her train. "Shan't be a minute," he said apologetically, and slipped out of the room.

The Doctor was studying the main control console. "Tell me, Mr. Grierson, does this console here control the angle of your radar dish?"

Grierson looked suspiciously at him. "Yes, it does, Doctor—why do you ask?"

"I've got a little scheme, Mr. Grierson—and I shall need your help."

Corporal Adams came along the corridor, just relieved from gate duty, his mind full of ham and eggs in the canteen. He turned a corner and saw someone in the corridor kneeling by a slumped body . . . Mr. Benton's body! He raised his gun to cover the kneeling figure. "What's going on here?"

The kneeling man turned and looked up at him and Adams gave a gasp of astonishment. The soldier leaning over Benton, was Benton . . . He opened his mouth to shout an alarm, and a savage blow struck him down from behind. The android technician caught the falling body and laid it down beside the body of the real Benton. The android Benton got to its feet, and gave a nod of satisfaction. "Good. Have then taken away. I shall go and dismiss the sentries at the main gate." It turned and headed for the entrance hall.

The Doctor finished explaining his plan to an ever more astonished Grierson. "There you are then. Now, could you do that for me?"

"Well, I could, Doctor. I mean it's theoretically possible. But it'll take time. I'd have to re-jig about eleven circuits."

"Then I suggest you get started at once—and tell no one, no one what you're doing."

Grierson dropped voice. "We can't do it, Doctor. If we point the radar dish downwards as you suggest and feed all our power into it, we'll jam every bit of radio and electronic equipment for miles around. There'll be utter chaos."

"Believe me, Mr. Grierson, nothing like the chaos there's going to be if you don't do it," whispered the Doctor. "Now, get moving, man."

Grierson opened his mouth to protest further, but before he could speak an angry Colonel Faraday burst red-faced into the room, towing Harry Sullivan behind him. "So, there you are,

Doctor! Now, do you mind telling me what all this is about?"

"It's about an invasion of Earth, Colonel Faraday. I suggest we go to your office. You've got some very important phone calls to make."

Calmly the Doctor led the way out of the room, talking as he went. "I've got some rather unpleasant news for you, Colonel. Crayford has sold you out to the Kraals."

Faraday hurried after him. "Kraals? Who the blazes are the Kraals?"

"An alien race bent on the conquest of Earth. They've evolved a very ingenious plan . . ."

The Doctor's voice faded as he disappeared along the corridor, trailing Harry Sullivan and Colonel Faraday behind him.

Grierson looked thoughtfully at the console that controlled the radar scanner dish. On the face of it the Doctor's request was absurd. But there had been something curiously compelling about him all the same. And it was an intriguing idea . . . Thoughtfully Grierson began removing an access panel from the console.

He looked up as Benton popped his head into the room. "Where's the Doctor?"

"Mr. Sullivan and the Colonel are back. They all went up to the Colonel's office."

The Benton android nodded, glancing round the room. Everything seemed in order. Just a technician busy at some minor repair job. It turned and went out into the corridor. There was much to do.

* * *

In Faraday's office the Doctor was finishing his explanations. He knew that Harry Sullivan would take the truth of his story on trust, but Faraday was still looking very doubtful. The Doctor wished desperately that Lethbridge-Stewart hadn't chosen this moment to go rushing off to Geneva. Most of the time the Brigadier was under his feet, and the one time he needed him the wretched fellow wasn't there.

As the Doctor finished, Faraday slumped lower behind his desk, muttering, "Kraals, androids . . . the whole thing's utterly fantastic."

Harry was fascinated by the Doctor's story. "You've seen these androids, Doctor? They really are good enough to pass for the real thing?"

"Indeed they are, Harry. You could chat to one for ages and never know."

"*I'd* know," growled Faraday. "I'm not going to have any aliens infiltrating my command."

"I wouldn't be too confident, Colonel," said the Doctor mischievously. "I happen to know they've made a replica of Harry. They've probably made one of you as well."

Harry looked alarmed. "If these android things are as good as the Doctor says, some of them might be amongst us already, without our knowing." He looked meaningly at the Colonel. "Tell you what, sir, I could run a medical check on everyone on the base. As soon as I

110

pass anyone, then we'll know they're all right."

Faraday was enthusiastic. "Good idea, my boy. What do you say, Doctor? Will that take care of your worries? I'll give Sullivan a special squad of men. He can vet the whole place for us."

"A proper medical examination of everybody would take too long. Luckily there's a short-cut." The Doctor produced a small torch-like device from his pocket.

Harry stared. "What is it?"

"It's a simple robot detector," said the Doctor proudly "The little bulb on the end lights up in the presence of an android. You use it like this." He pointed the instrument at Colonel Faraday. The bulb lit up.

There was a moment of silence. "Thing must be faulty," rumbled Faraday.

The Doctor shook his head. "No, I don't think so. It's pretty well foolproof." He pointed the device at himself. The bulb went out. He turned the instrument on Harry Sullivan. The bulb lit up again.

"I see," said the Doctor softly. "So, I was too late after all. The real Harry Sullivan and Colonel Faraday did go into that rocket—*and they're still there!* You two came back down in the elevator—two androids!"

From behind him an astonishingly familiar voice said, "A pity you had to find out, Doctor. We didn't really want any shooting until the takeover was complete."

111

The Doctor turned. Standing in the doorway he saw himself—a self that was covering him with a heavy revolver. Cheerfully the Doctor said, "Hullo, Doctor! We've been waiting for you."

He studied his other self with some admiration. "I must say the likeness is absolutely astonishing. For a moment I thought I was seeing double." Calmly the Doctor strolled up to the door and put his hand on the knob.

The android Doctor raised the revolver. "Keep back, Doctor!"

The Doctor smiled mockingly at his other self for a moment—then slammed the door into it, sending the android reeling into the corridor.

He whirled round and shoved the other two androids aside. Shielding his face with his arms, he took a flying leap, disappearing through the window in a shower of broken glass.

The Doctor landed on the lawn just below, thankful the Colonel's was a first-floor office. He rolled over, got to his feet and sprinted for the corner of the building. A bullet chipped stone from the wall beside him, and he glanced back to see the android Doctor firing from the window. Then he was round the corner and out of sight.

He found he was by the main gate—and Sarah was strolling innocently through it. Without even slowing his pace, the Doctor grabbed her by the arm and dragged her along after him. They ran round the side of the building

112

and eventually found shelter behind a concrete fuel bunker at the edge of the rocket field.

As they crouched down panting, the Doctor reached out and solemnly took Sarah's pulse. She stared at him. "What are you doing, Doctor? This is a funny time to worry about my health."

The Doctor grinned. "It's *my* health I'm worrying about, Sarah. I'm just making sure you're really you."

"Well, I know you're you all right, Doctor. I could hear them shooting at you. What's going on here?"

Colonel Faraday's voice echoed over the rocket field. "Attention all units. It has been confirmed that the person calling himself the Doctor is an imposter. He is attempting to sabotage the Research Center. He is believed to be at large in the area of the rocket field. A saturation search will begin immediately."

The Doctor looked at Sarah. "Does that answer your question?"

"We were too late. The androids have already taken over."

Faraday's voice boomed on. "This man is armed and dangerous. All military personnel are authorized to shoot on sight. That is all."

"What's happened to the real Colonel Faraday?"

The Doctor pointed to the rocket. "He's in there with the real Harry Sullivan. They're prisoners of Styggron—if they're still alive."

"Doctor, we've got to help them."

"We've also got to stop the Earth being taken over," pointed out the Doctor. "I'm going back inside the Center."

"Is there anything I can do to help?"

"Well, not really. It all depends on whether a chap called Grierson has done what I asked."

"Right. Then if you don't need me, I'm going to go and help Harry. I'll see you, Doctor."

Before the Doctor could stop her, Sarah was on her feet and running towards the rocket.

The Doctor sighed and got to his feet. He was as worried about Harry as Sarah was—but the fate of the entire Earth had to come first. Now, how was he going to get into the Center with a gang of armed androids hunting for him? Suddenly the Doctor smiled. By turning the enemy's strength against them of course, and taking advantage of the confusion they themselves were creating.

He got to his feet and walked confidently towards the Center. Deciding that the main entrance was too public, the Doctor walked round the edge of the building until he found a small side door unguarded. Once inside the sprawling building with its maze of corridors, he began working his way towards the scanner room.

Things went surprisingly well at first—he seemed to have chosen a relatively quiet area.

Suddenly the Doctor's luck ran out. He turned a corner and found himself face to face with Benton.

For a moment the Doctor had a wild hope that this was the real Benton, but he was soon disillusioned. The usually cheerful face was cold and hard, and a gun swung up to cover him.

The android cocked the gun with a metallic click. Helplessly the Doctor watched its finger tighten on the trigger . . .

12

Death of a Doctor

The Doctor remembered that all this had happened before. This time there would be no miracle to save him. Not unless he could manage one himself. He put a slight robotic stiffness into his movements, and deliberately flattened the tone of his voice. "Don't be a fool, Benton. Can't you see I'm one of you?" He walked straight towards the levelled gun.

The android Benton backed away, the gun still raised.

The Doctor continued his advance. "Didn't you hear the Colonel just now? The Doctor isn't in the building at all, he's over on the rocket field."

The gun muzzle was touching the Doctor's chest. He stared confidently into the android's face, and suddenly it lowered the gun and stepped back. "Sorry, sir."

The Doctor said casually, "That's all right. But keep your wits about you, Benton. Nobody knows who's who around here." Pleased with his little joke, the Doctor went on his way.

* * *

Sarah crouched by the foot of the rocket gantry, staring up at the black bulk looming above her. She looked longingly at the elevator. But using that would be bound to attract attention. Besides, she could scarcely go marching in the front door of the rocket and tell Styggron she'd come to release his prisoners. She needed some more secret entrance. Like the cargo hatch she and the Doctor had got through when the rocket was still on Oseidon. She could see the hatch now, but it looked terribly high above her. Still if she climbed up the gantry and reached across . . . Sarah shivered. She hated heights, and she'd done this climb once already. It didn't seem fair that she should have to do it again, without the Doctor to help her. Still, after announcing she was off to rescue Harry, she couldn't just cower in hiding until some passing android captured her. Screwing up her nerve, Sarah started to climb . . .

The Doctor hurried into the control room just as Grierson was making a final circuit connection. "Have you finished?"

Grierson went on working. "Almost there."

"Hurry, man," urged the Doctor. "There isn't a second to lose."

Grierson finished the re-connection and replaced the access hatch. "There, that does it. I

117

just have to switch on full power." He crossed to a master power-switch on a nearby panel. As his hand touched the switch a shot rang out. He staggered and fell, clutching his shoulder.

The Doctor whirled round. The android Doctor stood in the doorway, revolver in hand. "A clever way to jam android control circuits, Doctor. But I'm afraid you weren't quick enough."

The Doctor went to kneel beside Grierson. The wound was a bad one but perhaps not fatal. He ripped off the edge of Grierson's white coat and made a pad to put over the wound.

He straightened up to face his android self— and it raised its revolver. The doors opened and Crayford hurried into the room. Quickly he took in the scene, the wounded Grierson, and the android Doctor covering the real one with its revolver. "What's going on here?"

Emotionlessly the android said, "I am about to dispose of the Doctor. He has interfered in out plans for the last time."

Crayford stepped between them. "No! Styggron promised me there would be no unnecessary killing."

"You are a fool, Crayford," said the android Doctor coldly. "Do you really thing the Kraals will spare humanity? Styggron has a virus on board that ship that will kill every man, woman and child in the world."

How strange, thought the Doctor, that an android should take such pride in the ruthlessness of its creator. Yet perhaps it was natural. Created by Kraal technology, such values and emotions as it had were those of Kraals. The Doctor's eyes were fixed on Crayford's face. The humanity in Crayford was beginning to break free of the Kraal conditioning. In that reviving humanity lay the Doctor's only chance of escape.

An expression of horror came over Crayford's face. "No, I don't believe you. Styggron wouldn't do that. He's a surgeon, a healer. Look at what he did for me." As always at moments of stress, Crayford rubbed his hand nervously over the black eye-patch.

The Doctor raised his voice. "Styggron did nothing for you, Crayford. Nothing whatsoever, except brainwash you!"

Crayford stared wildly at him. "It's not true." He turned to the android. "Tell me it's not true."

The android said nothing. It stood there patiently, waiting for Crayford to move so that it could kill the Doctor. It had no objection to killing Crayford first, but as yet it had not been instructed to do so.

"You were hijacked by the Kraals," shouted the Doctor. "They drew your ship off course. Nothing went wrong with your rocket, and you were never healed by the Kraals because you were never injured. Take off that eyepatch and look for yourself."

Crayford could see his own face reflected

clearly in a nearby monitor screen. Slowly his hand went up to the eye-patch.

The Doctor waited, hoping desperately that his guess was correct. He had felt all along that the story of the missing eye had been no more than a detail invented to convince Crayford that he owed the Kraals his life.

Staring at his reflection, Crayford ripped away the patch. From the screen, two perfectly good eyes looked back at him. For a moment Crayford stood frozen. Then he gave a scream of desperate rage. "Styggron!" he screamed, and ran from the room.

For a second the android was distracted. The Doctor's foot shot out in a beautifully timed kick, smashing the gun from its hand. Instantly the android leaped for him, and the Doctor found himself in a nightmare struggle with himself.

The worst of it was that he had no chance of winning. The Doctor himself had more than human strength but he was fighting a machine, a creature of metal and plastic, an enemy who would never tire and could not be hurt.

The android's hands were reaching for his throat and it took all the Doctor's strength to keep them away. He smashed his arms upwards to break the android's grip, broke free, and made for the power switch. The android caught him and flung him back, sending him staggering across the room. Calmly the android pressed an alarm button on the wall and a bell beside it began an ear-splitting clangor. Then it attacked the Doctor again, grappling with him as he rose and made another desperate lunge for the power switch. Locked in each other's arms the two Doctors, real and android, staggered across the room.

All over the complex, androids heard the alarm signal, and guessed its significance. The android Benton, Harry Sullivan and Colonel Faraday, android soldiers and android technicians, all ran towards the scanner room.

The Faraday, Benton and Sullivan androids arrived first, android soldiers close behind them. They stood in the doorway watching the final struggle. They made no attempt to interfere, knowing their fellow-android's victory was only a matter of time.

With a last desperate effort, the Doctor broke free again, the android leaped at him, the Doctor dodged, tripped it and lunged for the power-switch. As his fingers grasped it the android's hands clamped round his throat. The fingers tightened and the Doctor heaved on the switch, dragging it down with his own weight as he slumped to the ground.

As the power-relay snapped home the fingers choking the Doctor released their hold. The android Doctor fell twisting and writhing to the floor. It thrashed about for a moment and then lay still. Exactly the same thing happened to the other androids in the room, a flurry of uncontrolled movement, followed by total collapse.

Rubbing his throat tenderly, the Doctor got slowly to his feet. He looked down at his android self as it lay crumpled on the floor.

Grierson stirred and moaned, and the Doctor went over to him. "Are you all right?"

"I think so." Grierson looked round the body-littered room. "What happened to them?"

"We jammed their circuits," said the Doctor happily. He looked round the room. "Where's Crayford?"

"No idea," said Grierson painfully. "He suddenly rushed off. He was shouting about someone called Styggron."

The Doctor nodded. "I was forgetting him. I'd better get over to the rocket."

The Doctor went over to the door and then he paused. His hand went to his pocket, searching for his sonic screwdriver.

After a long and hazardous climb, much of it with her eyes shut, Sarah managed to wriggle through the cargo hatch. She found herself in the cargo hold she'd shared with the Doctor. Colonel Faraday and Harry Sullivan were tied up on the floor.

"Harry!" said Sarah happily. She went across to him and began unwrapping the plastic bonds.

Harry said delightedly. "Sarah, old girl! What on earth is going on?"

Sarah grinned. "It's a very long story, Harry. Did you know you had a very nasty twin?"

"Twin?" Harry stared blankly at her.

"That's right. An android Harry. It keeps trying to kill me!"

She finished untying him, and went to help Colonel Faraday.

"What's all this about androids, young lady?" he spluttered.

"They're robots, duplicates of people on Earth. The Doctor will explain . . ."

As Sarah finished untying Faraday she heard a noise behind her and turned.

Styggron was covering her with a blaster. He seemed even more astonished than she was. "The enterprising Earth girl." Sarah stepped forward and he raised the weapon. "No, don't move. This is a neutron blaster, it will annihilate you immediately. I heard the sounds of an intruder. I hardly expected to find it was you."

"I suppose you thought I was still a prisoner on your rotten planet!"

Styggron shook his massive head in amazement. "I know the Doctor managed to escape. I constructed an android of him as a precaution. But you—you must indeed have a charmed life."

"What are you babbling about Styggron?"

"You were to have been the first human victim of the virus that will destroy all humanity."

He held up a sealed phial. "See, it is here. How did you escape the virus? Did you not drink the water?"

"Water?" Sarah was horrified. "You mean that water you sent me in the cell was infected?"

Crayford appeared in the doorway behind Styggron. Sarah saw with surprise that he wore no eye-patch, and his other eye seemed perfectly all right.

Crayford's face was white and his eyes glittered feverishly. Sarah thought he looked like a man on the point of total breakdown. "You have betrayed me, Styggron!" he screamed.

Styggron laughed. "Betrayed you, Crayford? I used you, as I use the androids. But I fear you are no longer of any value to me." He raised his blaster.

With the courage of madness, Crayford jumped on him, knocking the blaster aside, and sending the phial flying from Styggron's hand.

With a bellow of rage, Styggron flung Crayford away and fired. The force of the neutron blast slammed Crayford's dead body into the corner of the hold.

As Styggron swung the blaster to cover Sarah and the others a tall figure appeared in the doorway behind him. "Doctor!" screamed Sarah. "Look out!" Before Styggron could turn, an arm took him around the throat. The Doctor's other hand reached in front of Styggron, trying to get a grip on the neutron blaster.

124

With a roar of rage the Kraal broke free. He jumped back to get a clear shot but as he did so, a foot shot out to trip him. Styggron crashed over backwards. His head thudded down onto the phial of virus solution which had rolled unnoticed into the corner.

The impact of Styggron's massive skull shattered the phial. A pool of colorless liquid spread around his head. The effect of the virus in its concentrated form was immediate and terrible. Styggron's head began to *dissolve,* like a ball of wax in a roaring flame. Soon it was a shapeless, horrible blob. Such was the strength in the stocky figure that the dying Kraal's body thrashed about for a moment longer. By some dying reflex, its finger tightened on the trigger. The blaster fired and the full force of its impact took the tall figure standing above him full in the chest. It crumpled and lay still.

"No," sobbed Sarah. "No! Oh Doctor!" She was kneeling to examine the fallen body, when a familiar voice said, "Spare no tears for him, Sarah. He was only an android!"

Sarah looked up. Standing in the doorway was the Doctor, miraculously unhurt. He pointed to the huddled shape beside her. "That was only my replica—an android."

Sarah still couldn't take it in. "An android," she said dazedly. "But it attacked Styggron."

"I fitted it with a shielding device and then reprogrammed it," said the Doctor. "I decided to turn one of their own weapons against them."

Sarah straightened up. "Please, Doctor, don't ever do anything like that again! One of you's quite enough!"

The Doctor smiled and helped her to her feet. There was still much to be done. The immobilized androids would have to be collected and dismantled before the low level scanner beam could be switched off. But soon life in the Space Research Center—and in Devesham village—would return to normal. Marshal Chedaki would wait in vain for Styggron's signal to bring the invasion fleet of the Kraals to an unsuspecting Earth. With Styggron dead, his master plan had come to nothing. The android invasion was over.